also by
alyson noël

Dreamland

A Riley Bloom Book

alyson noël

SQUARE
FISH

St. Martin's Griffin
New York

For Dorice—the Ever to my Riley!

A SQUARE FISH BOOK
An Imprint of Macmillan

Library of Congress Cataloging-in-Publication Data Available

ISBN 978-0-312-56375-2

First Edition: September 2011

Square Fish logo designed by Filomena Tuosto

Cover design by Angela Goddard

Cover illustration by Juliana Kolesova

Flowers and grass © Gerald Nowak/photolibrary; tree © Shutterstock

Book designed by Susan Walsh

mackids.com

10 9 8 7 6 5 4 3 2 1

Soul Catcher [sōl] catch·er [káchər, kéchər] *n* One who catches the lost souls that haunt the earth plane by coaxing and convincing them to cross the bridge to the Here & Now.

There is nothing to fear but fear itself.

—franklin d. roosevelt

I

The second I laid eyes on Aurora my shoulders slumped, my face unsquinched, and I heaved a deep sigh of relief knowing I had an ally, a friend on my side.

I was sure it would all be okay.

It was in the way her hair shimmered and shone—transforming from yellow to brown to black to red before starting the sequence all over again.

Her skin did the same, converting from the palest white to the darkest ebony, and every possible hue in between.

And her gown, her gorgeous yellow gown, sparkled and gleamed and swished at her feet like a crush of fallen stars.

Even though I no longer mistook her for an angel like I did the first time I saw her, still, the whole glistening sight calmed me in a major way.

But, as it turns out, I'd misread the whole thing.

As soon as I took one look at her aura—as soon as I noted

the way its usual bright, popping purple had dimmed to a much duller violet—well, that's when I knew we were on opposite sides.

It was just like Bodhi had said: I had a heckuva lot to explain. My last Soul Catch hadn't exactly been assigned.

I stared at my feet, head hanging in shame, scraggly blond hair hanging limply before me as I forced myself to shuffle behind him. Using those last remaining moments to run a frantic search through my best, most plausible excuses—mentally rehearsing my story again and again like a panicky actor on opening night.

Even though I'd only been doing my job as a Soul Catcher when I coaxed and convinced a whole lot of ghosts to cross the bridge to where they belonged, there was no denying the fact that I'd been told to look the other way—to mind my own business. To not get involved by sticking my semi-stubby nose in places where it most certainly didn't belong.

But did I listen?

Uh, not exactly.

Instead I charged full speed ahead into a whole heap of trouble.

I followed Bodhi to the stage, his back so stiff and his hands so clenched I was glad I couldn't see his face. Though, if I had to guess, I'd be willing to bet that his mouth, free of the straw he usually chomped when the Council wasn't around, was pinched into a thin, grim line, while his green eyes, heavily shadowed by his insanely thick fringe of lashes, were sparking and flaring as he thought of ways to rid himself of me once and for all.

I peered under my bangs, watching as Aurora took her place next to Claude, who sat next to Samson, who was right beside Celia, who was so tiny and petite she was able to share an armrest with Royce without either one of them having to compromise or fight for equal space. And seeing them all assembled like that, waiting to hear just how I might go about explaining myself, well, that's when I remembered the most important evidence of all.

The one undeniable thing that required no verbal explanation, as it was right there smack dab in the front and center, visible for all to see.

I had my glow on.

Actually, scratch that. It wasn't just my usual glow. It was far more impressive than that.

As a reward for all I'd accomplished my glow had significantly deepened. Going from what started out as a barely there, pale green shimmer straight into a . . . well . . . a somewhat deeper green shimmer.

Okay, maybe the change wasn't all that drastic, but the thing is, what it lacked in drama it made up for in substance.

Let's just say that it couldn't be missed.

After all, I'd seen it.

Bodhi had seen it.

Even Buttercup had looked right at me and barked a few times as he wagged his tail and spun around.

All of which I took as a pretty good sign that the Council would see it too—from what I knew of them, they didn't miss a thing.

I relaxed, pushed my hair off my face, and thought: *How bad can it be when my glow is so clearly minty green?*

But then I remembered what Bodhi had said about consequences and actions—about the Council's ability to give and take at will. Insisting that because of my failure to follow orders, it was really quite possible that by the time we were done, neither of us would ever glow again.

Knowing I had to act fast, do whatever it took to get them to see my side of things, I charged straight ahead.

I had no time for trouble. No time to waste.

Just moments before I'd learned something extraordinary—had heard about some mysterious dimension where all the dreams take place—and I was determined to find it.

Besides, I was pretty sure Bodhi couldn't be trusted. The fact that he found me a burden wasn't a secret.

When it came right down to it, it was every man, er,

make that *ghost,* for himself. So I squeezed him right out and took center stage.

He gasped in astonishment. Tried to push me away. But he was too late, and I was too fast, and before he could do anything more, I was already standing smack dab in front of the Council, pushing aside any lingering fear.

Fear was for sissies. Of that I was sure.

It was time for me to tell them my side of things.

My story. My way.

And I was just about to begin, when I noticed the way Aurora's aura grew dimmer, as the rest of the Council's followed suit. Darkening in a way that made my mouth grow so dry, and my throat go so lumpy, the words jammed in my throat.

I stood shaking. Mute. Watching as Bodhi—my guide—the one person whose job it was to help me—shook his head and smirked. Leaving no doubt in my mind just how much he'd enjoy watching me burn.

2

The next thing I knew, Bodhi had leaped right before me, and said, "Hi!"

Chasing it with a dazzling smile—one that showcased his dimples and made his eyes gleam. And as if that weren't enough, he then shifted in a way that shamelessly allowed a chunk of wavy brown hair to fall into those eyes and tangle with his extra thick lashes—just so he could sweep his bangs off his face and smile again.

It was a Hollywood move.

Slick.

Superficial.

Spurious (thank you, word-a-day calendar!) in the very worst way.

The kind of move that either makes your heart flutter, or makes you go *blech*. And seeing Bodhi do it, well, it just made me feel weird.

But when the move didn't win him the reaction he'd hoped, when the members of the Council didn't swoon all over themselves, he shifted gears, cleared his voice, and looking directly at them, uttered a very serious-sounding "Hello."

To be honest, I was a little embarrassed by the double greeting, but before I could do anything to stop him he said, "As you know, Riley, Buttercup, and I ran into a little trouble recently, and . . ."

He rambled.

Oh boy, did he ramble.

He rambled in a way that was nothing but a bunch of bippidy blah blah to my ears.

Rambled in a way that made my head go all dizzy and squeezy.

Rambled in a way that wasn't the least bit effective—or at least not where the Council was concerned. And I knew I had to stop him before it got any worse. So the second he paused, I jumped in to say, "I think what Bodhi means is—"

He swung toward me, glaring in a way that was half rage, half horrified disbelief. But it wasn't enough to stop me. Not even close.

But before I could even get started, Royce, with the dark wavy hair, smooth dark skin, and glinting green eyes that amounted to the kind of breath-stealing good looks usually reserved for movie screens, said, "That's enough, Riley."

I froze—too afraid to look at Bodhi—too afraid to look at anyone—those three simple words stopping me cold. Not once in my ridiculously brief twelve years of life had I heard that phrase used for anything other than to stop me from some type of behavior an adult found extremely annoying.

An awkward pause followed, broken by Celia, who stood beside Royce, her usual cornflower blue glow once again beaming at full force when she said, "There is no need to continue. No need to make excuses or explain. We have seen everything."

I nodded. Gulped. It was all I could do.

My eyes locking on Samson's deep violet ones as his hands clasped either side of his seat. "You acted on your own. You acted willfully, wildly, you ignored Bodhi's instructions, and put yourselves in great danger." He rose to his feet and stood rigid before me. "In the future we ask that you consult with us first before you go off on your own. No matter where you find yourself on the earth plane, you must never forget that we are but one telepathic message away."

He shot me a stern look, Bodhi too, the two of us frozen, unsure what to do, when Aurora said, "There is no need to fear us. We are here to offer guidance, support, and assistance if you find that you need it. And while I know you are eager to advance, you must trust that each and every assignment has been carefully selected to match your level of progress." Her gaze locked on mine, making sure I understood, before she went on to add, "That said, you have still managed to succeed where many other Soul Catchers have failed. Congratulations."

Bodhi softened, as a whistle of air I didn't even know I'd been holding escaped from my lips. And when I glanced down at Buttercup, I watched as he raised his rump high and let loose in a flurry of wiggles—an overdose of cuteness. I found myself wishing he'd stop.

There was no need to overdo it. Not when I'd just been acknowledged—no, scratch that—not when I'd just been *congratulated* by Aurora, who I was pretty sure was the Council's queen bee.

I'd put myself in danger. I'd taken great risks. I'd done the exact opposite of what Bodhi had ordered—and look where it got me:

Glowing before the Council.

Graciously accepting great praise.

Congratulations!

The word spun through my head.

I wasn't in trouble. All was okay. Actually, it was better than okay. Once again, I'd succeeded where others had failed.

I knew it.

The Council knew it.

And my glow proved it.

It was Bodhi who needed the attitude adjustment. Me—I was at the top of my game.

I reveled in my success, reliving the praise over and over again.

My thoughts interrupted by the melodic lilt of Aurora's voice when she added, "It is obvious that you are in need of greater challenges in the future, so we will do our best to provide them for you."

I nodded, arranging my face into the perfect expression of humility, saving the victory dance for later.

My attention was soon stolen by Claude, whose long, slim fingers fiddled with the scraggly beard that stopped just shy of his waist, as he said, "And so, in light of all that you have accomplished, we agree that you two are in need of a break."

I glanced at Bodhi, taking a sidelong peek at the brand-spanking-new sneakers I was sure he'd manifested just for this meeting, the dark denim jeans that pooled around his ankles in that cool-guy way, his slouchy blue sweater that skimmed his lean form, making my way up to his ridiculously cute face, which, just the sight of it alone, caused my throat to go all lumpy and hot as an unexpected wave of nostalgia for all that we'd shared threatened to swallow me whole.

As much as I'd longed for a new guide (pretty much since the moment Bodhi and I met), just when I was about to get one, well, I could hardly believe our days of Soul Catching together were coming to such a quick end. After this meeting, we might never see each other again.

For some strange reason, the thought didn't spark the kind of joy I would've expected. If anything, it did just the opposite. It made me feel all twisty and turvy and a little bit empty.

But, as it turns out, I was wrong.

Dead wrong.

The Council had other ideas.

"Take a break from Soul Catching," Aurora said, nodding in a way that made her hair dance and swirl. "Take some time to relax and enjoy yourselves."

My face squinched, unsure how to take that.

I mean, hadn't I just been congratulated?

And didn't that sort of praise mean I could skip a few grades and move on to the kind of big, scary ghosts the experienced Soul Catchers dealt with?

It was Celia who set me straight. "While we are all quite delighted with your performance, Riley, and while it's clear that we'll need to find greater challenges for you, we think you could use some time off." Her tiny hands fluttered at her waist like a hummingbird before a feeder. "And once you're sufficiently refreshed, we'll happily send you and Bodhi on your next assignment. We are delighted with the way you two work together. Clearly you bring out the best in each other."

I gaped. And I'm talkin' the bug-eyed, jaw-to-the-knees kind of gaped. I mean, seriously? *Bring out the best in each other?* Was she kidding? Had any of them actually reviewed the footage of Bodhi and me attempting to work together?

All we did was fight!

And argue.

And willfully oppose each other every chance that we got.

The only times we ever pitched in, rolled up our sleeves, and put our vast and varied differences aside was after things were so far gone we had no other choice but to rely on each other.

But apparently that wasn't all. Oh, no, they were a long way from done, because right as I was still reeling from that, Royce piped in and said, "While we take some time in choosing your next assignment, you and Bodhi, and yes, even you, Buttercup—" Royce's eyes sparkled when Buttercup, upon hearing his name, licked his chops and wiggled his rump once again. "—you should all enjoy your time off. Spend some time with family. Visit with friends. The important thing is for you to rest up and recharge. Don't worry, we'll find you when it's time for your next assignment. But for now, you are released."

Released.

Freed.

Undeniably dismissed.

And yet, even though I'd heard every word, all I could do was just stand there and gawk, watching as Bodhi and Buttercup shot across the stage and made a mad dash for the door. Suddenly paralyzed by the horrible realization that, unlike me, they had other, better places to be.

The Council had vanished—just *poof* and they were gone. And knowing it was lame (not to mention pathetic) to keep standing there long after everyone else had vacated, I hung my head low and retraced Bodhi's and Buttercup's steps.

The dismal truth of my existence blooming before me: While I may have excelled at Soul Catching, I was a total failure when it came to having an afterlife.

My social life was even deader than I.

I had no friends. No hobbies. No place to go other than my own room.

And while it's true that my parents and grandparents were Here, it's also true that they were busy with their own afterlives.

The Here & Now was nothing like the earth plane. I didn't need anyone to pay my bills, prepare my meals, sign permission slips, drive me around, or just generally look after me in a shelter-food-and-money kind of way. Everything I could possibly want, and/or need, could be had simply by wishing it—which meant that other than dropping by to check in and say hi, my family was no longer responsible for me.

They'd moved on.

And the pathetic truth was, from what I'd seen, my grandparents were way more popular than I.

I slammed through the door and hurled myself outside, determined to do whatever it took to get myself an afterlife.

3

The first thing I saw when I pushed through the door was that Bodhi and Buttercup had waited for me.

Bodhi leaned against the iron stair rail, a dented green straw wedged between his back teeth, while Buttercup sat at his feet, tongue lolling out the side of his mouth.

I ran toward them, dropped to my knees, and hunched my shoulders 'til I was nose to nose with my dog. Giving him a good, long scratch between the ears, and smiling when he closed his eyes and sunk his head low, feeling just as contented as he. So immersed in the moment, so overcome with the thrill of them waiting, that all of my earlier sadness melted away.

While it was true that I didn't have much of an afterlife, at least I wouldn't have to go it alone.

I cleared my throat, knowing I should say something nice. Nothing too mushy, I'd never been comfortable with that sort of thing, but still, I wanted to show the full extent of my gratitude. Let them know how happy I was to find them both there.

My lips parting, just about to speak, when I saw the way Bodhi's knee jiggled—the way his thumbs tapped hard and fast against the rail—and I knew I'd misjudged the whole thing.

Bodhi had no interest in hanging with me. He was still in guide mode. Waiting was an act of duty.

Perhaps even pity.

He was just making sure I had somewhere to be—that I wouldn't make any more trouble—so he could head off on his much-anticipated vacation with no further thoughts of me.

I was the very last item on his to-do list.

A terrible realization that made all the nice words die right on my tongue. While the words that sprang up to replace them were anything but.

"So," I said, still petting Buttercup as my gaze fixed hard on Bodhi. "The Council seemed pretty dang happy with all of my accomplishments. Bet that came as a big shock to you, huh?" I paused, waited for him to reply, hoping he'd volley right back with something sarcastic so I could return it with something even worse.

I was looking for a fight. There was no getting around it.

Mostly because I would not, could not, stand for him to pity me. That just wouldn't do.

Bodhi squinted, stared at me for a good long bit. And when he did finally speak, his voice was so casual you'd think he'd misunderstood the tone of my words. "Why do you say that?" he asked, the green straw sliding across his front teeth.

"Um, maybe because they *congratulated me*?" I said, stealing a moment to tack on a nice, dramatic eye roll to go with it. My energy growing so heated, so riled up and angry, it wasn't long before Buttercup whined and scooted away from me.

But if Bodhi was fazed, he sure didn't show it. Instead he just laughed. Well, it was actually more of a cross between a laugh, a huff, and a grunt, but anyway, he just made a sound, tucked the straw in the side of his mouth, and said, "No, what I meant was, why did you say that bit about my not being happy for your accomplishments?"

"Uh, because you're not?" I made a face, frowning even more as I watched Buttercup scooch closer to Bodhi and farther from me.

Bodhi shrugged, gazed all around, as his knee picked up the tempo, jiggling so fast it practically blurred.

And that's when I got it.

That's when I completely understood.

It was worse than I'd thought.

Bodhi hadn't been waiting for me. This had nothing to do with me. He'd been waiting for someone else to catch up with him.

I swear, if I'd still been alive, that would've been the exact moment when my cheeks would've burned so bright I would've had no choice but to run and hide. But, as it was, I stayed put, looking at him when I said, "Surely you remember what you said just before we came here? That because of me, because of my insistence on disobeying your rules—'we may never glow again.' You said that the Council can 'give and take at will.' You said all of that, and yet, check it out—I still got my glow on!"

I thrust my arm toward him, hoping he'd take a good look. But it was no use. His attention was claimed. He was already moving away.

I watched as he ran a hand over his hair and his clothes. Trying to appear jaunty, self-assured, totally and completely in control, but I knew him well enough to know better. He was making a colossal effort to hide a major case of nerves.

Though it's not like *she* noticed.

Oh, no. She was too busy swinging her long, shiny black braids. Too busy adjusting her sweater and straightening her short, pleated skirt. Too busy smiling, and waving, and looking really cute.

And even though I should've known, even though I

should've guessed by the way she shouted and catcalled the loudest at that weird graduation ceremony I attended when I first got Here, I had no idea that the girl I'd mentally referred to as cheerleader girl (mostly because of the cheerleading outfit she always wears)—I had no idea that she and Bodhi were friends.

I guess I was hoping she and I could be friends.

But now it was clear that was not meant to be.

And just when I thought I couldn't feel any lower, I watched Buttercup race toward them like the worst kind of traitor.

I shoved two fingers into my mouth and whistled for him to return.

And when he didn't, when he completely ignored me, I whistled again.

And when he still didn't return, I manifested a handful of his very favorite doggy biscuits as a bribe—praying it would work, and feeling ridiculously relieved when it did.

He slumped toward me, snatched the biscuits right off my palm, then turned away to eat them, as though I couldn't be trusted. As though I might change my mind and try to yank them right back, even though I'd never done so before.

I knelt by his side, watching Bodhi and cheerleader girl talk, and laugh, and use any excuse they could think of to tap each other on the shoulder, the arm, the hand. A scene that reminded me of the times I used to spy on my big sister, Ever, and her boyfriend. Telling myself I was merely studying for when it would be my turn to be a teen—that I wasn't invading her privacy—remembering how they acted the very same way.

And if I thought my insides felt bad before, watching Bodhi and cheerleader girl flirt with each other, well, it left me feeling all hollow and weird.

Sure I could manifest the same shiny, pink lip gloss that made her lips gleam.

Sure I could braid my hair with the same kind of glistening beads that chimed like bells every time she flicked her head from side to side.

Heck, I could even manifest my own cheerleading outfit— all I had to do was envision it and it was as good as mine. Easy-peasy.

But I could never fill the sweater like she did.

I would never look as good in the skirt.

I would never look anything like her.

She was gorgeous, exotic, and when she wore a bra she managed to fill it.

Unlike me, she was a *teen*.

She was as opposite of lanky-haired, semi-stubby-nosed, blue-eyed, flat-chested me as you could get.

And there was nothing I could do about it.

I was stuck.

Eternally stuck.

Or, at least, that's what I thought until I remembered what Bodhi had recently said: "You have no idea how it works, do you?" His eyes had locked on mine. "No one is ever *stuck* anywhere, Riley. Seriously, what kind of a place do you think the Here & Now is?"

I'd gaped. At first unable to utter the words, though it wasn't long before I'd said, "You mean, I can . . . I can, maybe . . . actually . . . *turn thirteen someday?*"

I'd pressed my lips together, sure it was too good to be true. It was all I'd ever wanted. All I'd ever dreamed. And from the moment I died in the accident, I'd been sure the possibility had died along with me.

But Bodhi just quirked his brow and shrugged in a vague, noncommittal kind of way. "There're no limits that I'm aware of—pretty much anything is possible," he'd said, refusing to give any details, keeping the statement purposely hazy, and yet, he'd said it all the same. And at that moment, watching the glorious cheerleader girl standing before me, well, I clung to those words like a drowning man to a life raft.

Bodhi hooked his thumb over his shoulder and jabbed it toward me, causing cheerleader girl to cup her hands around either side of her mouth and call, "Good on you, Riley Bloom! I see you got your glow on!"

Oh, great. Talk about bad to worse. Not only did she have to go and remind me of just how nice she was, but up until she'd spoken I'd forgotten all about her accent.

It was crisp, and proper, and totally British.

She was pretty much as cool as they came.

I was ready to leave. Ready to cut my losses and *vámanos* myself right out of that place before my humiliation could get any worse, when Bodhi strode toward me and said, "Listen, Riley, Jasmine and I are taking off."

My eyes widened. *Jasmine?* Her name was *Jasmine?* I shook my head and sighed. But of course she'd get a cool, girly name while I got stuck with one usually reserved just for boys.

"You okay?" Bodhi's eyes flashed with a combination of impatience and concern, and to be honest, I just couldn't take it anymore.

I looked away, my voice awful and grumpy when I said, "Why wouldn't I be?" Words that surely failed to make me look any more mature in his eyes. His lips went flat, his face grew grim, and when he glanced over his shoulder at Jasmine with an impatient gaze, I couldn't help but add, "So why don't you just go already? I mean, *sheesh,* it's not like I need you to babysit me!"

His gaze narrowing so much his eyes became mere slashes of green. "So, where you headed?" he asked, but not because he was interested. But because as my guide, he pretty much had no choice but to keep tabs.

I frowned, thinking I should tell him that it's none of his business—that I was under no obligation to check in with him every second of the day. But instead I found myself saying, "I'm going to check out the place where all the dreams are created." Deciding then and there it was as good a destination as any.

He swung his head toward me, his face all outraged and screwy when he said, "What did you say?"

I shrugged, picked at the hem of my sweater, took my sweet time to answer. "You know, the place where all the dreams are created? I thought it sounded cool, so I figured I'd check it out. Why? Have you been?"

He groaned. Mashed his lips so hard they turned white at the edges. Then after glancing over his shoulder yet again, flashing Jasmine the *just a minute* signal, he turned back to me and said, "Listen, Riley, you can't go there. It's off-limits."

I was tempted to scoff. Tempted to remind him that we were on a break, which meant that, for the time being anyway, he was no longer the boss of me. But since all I knew about the place was what little I'd learned from the two old guys who first mentioned it back in the Viewing Room, I decided to quash my first instinct and play it another way.

"Why?" I asked, eyes widening in the way that always worked on my dad but rarely, if ever, on my mom.

"It's forbidden. Seriously. It's been outlawed for . . ." He pinched his brow, looked all around as if he expected to find the answer written somewhere. "Well, let's just say it's outlawed. But leave it to you to try to find it." He shook his head, slid a hand deep into his scalp where he clutched a fistful of hair, and sighed in frustration. "Just—just stay away, okay? Just this once, just, please, take my word for it, and do as I say. Can you do that? Can you behave yourself long enough for me to enjoy my hard-earned break?"

I screwed my mouth to the side, deciding to make him wait for my reply. Enjoying the fact that he was no longer checking on Jasmine—I finally had his full, undivided attention.

But it didn't take long before his knee started to jiggle, and this time, his fingers joined in. Twitching and fidgeting as they jumped from his hair to his sweater to his belt loop and back, eager to be rid of me—eager to move on to the kinds of things older kids did.

So I let him.

I gave him exactly what he wanted when I looked at him and said, "No worries. Forget I ever asked."

He shot me a skeptical look.

"Seriously." I nodded. "I mean, at first I thought it might

be kind of cool, but hey, if it's been outlawed and all, well . . ." I paused, taking a moment to rearrange my expression in a way that I hoped looked more honest. "I don't want to cause any more trouble. Not after getting big kudos from the Council, so . . ." I spun on my heel, hoping for a speedy exit, but it wasn't long before I realized Buttercup had, once again, chosen Bodhi over me. Forcing me to stop long enough to manifest another handful of dog biscuits just to get him to follow.

"Riley—this is for real, right? You're *not* just saying that, you meant what you said?" Bodhi's voice drifted behind me.

But I just stormed straight ahead, waving my hand in dismissal. Wanting him to think I was in a big hurry.

Wanting him to think I had somewhere far more exciting to be.

4

As it turned out, I didn't go to the place where all the dreams are created. And not just because of what Bodhi had said.

I mean, yeah, I'd heard him loud and clear. The place was outlawed. Forbidden. Or at least it was according to him. But besides the fact that it wouldn't do me any good to go looking for trouble, the main reason I didn't go was because I had no idea where to find it. No idea where to even begin.

So I went home instead. Figuring I'd just hang there until I came up with a much better plan. Not the least bit surprised to find the house empty. I pretty much expected it to be.

The house wasn't there for my parents or grandparents— the house was manifested for me.

My family had been in the Here & Now for a while. My grandparents having arrived way back when I was still a baby, while my parents came straight over from the scene of the accident.

I'm the one who lingered.

I'm the one who couldn't stand to leave my old life behind.

Still, from the moment I crossed the bridge and ended up Here, they were all waiting to greet me. Eager to show me around, show me the ropes, and one of the first things they did was bring me to an exact replica of our old house—thinking I'd be comforted by something familiar.

For a while it worked. I felt comforted for sure.

I loved the way my dad's old leather chair sat smack in the middle of the den just like it did in our original house back in Oregon. I loved the way Ever's and my initials were still carved into its arm (even though we got in some serious trouble for doing that). I loved the way Buttercup's leash hung on the wall, and how our mud-covered rain boots were all piled up against the back door. I even loved the way Ever's old room stayed exactly the same, allowing me to visit from time to time and gaze at her things. Pretending that, for the moment anyway, she wasn't so far away.

But mostly I loved my room.

I loved the way the walls were littered with the exact same posters I'd had back when I was alive.

I loved the way my dresser was crammed full of the

same kind of socks, and underwear, and cute T-shirts I once wore.

And while I hadn't been Here all that long, and while they'd gone to a great deal of effort to make it look lived in, I was pretty dang sure they hadn't spent any real time there before I came along.

I was pretty dang sure they had their own homes.

I mean, once you understand how it all works—once you understand that you can have the kind of house you always dreamed of merely by wishing it—well, most people wouldn't dream of settling for what they could afford back on the earth plane.

Most people set themselves up in places far more exciting than that.

Even though my entire street was made to look exactly like my old street back home, all you had to do was walk a few blocks and you'd find yourself among big stone castles, sprawling bungalows that seemed to go on forever, and all-glass, oceanfront places as big as resorts.

I guess most people adapt better than I have.

I guess most people dream bigger—dream beyond what used to be.

But back when I first arrived, I couldn't see it like that. I couldn't imagine anything better than what I'd had in the past.

Though clearly things were beginning to change, and there was no doubt I was changing too. So I did something I'd never done before—I plopped onto my bed and looked at my room with a critical eye—trying to see it as though it was the very first time.

Trying to see it through the eyes of cheerleader girl, Bodhi, or some other teen.

And the bad news was—it looked childish.

Maybe even—babyish.

Lacking in sophistication and style, for sure.

I mean, yeah, I still liked the same pop stars and celebrities whose pictures were taped to my walls. Heck, I still liked my bedspread and the big pile of shiny, fuzzy pillows that hogged so much space they threatened to spill onto the floor. I even liked most of my furniture too.

But that wasn't the point.

The point was that my room, no matter how much I still liked it, belonged to the twelve-year-old version of me—*not* the teen I was determined to be.

It was like lugging your baby blanket along on your first day of school—it was time to toss out the old and move on with the new.

I gazed all around, wondering where to begin. Then, in a fit of inspiration, I squinched my eyes shut, and when I opened them again, I found myself sprawled in the middle of a huge canopy bed with purple velvet drapes that swooped down from either side, and a big gold crown perched high at the top—just like the one I'd once seen on TV.

Buttercup stood in the doorway, his disapproving nose pitched high into the air, refusing to step onto the leopard-print carpet, and whining in a way that tugged at my heart.

Knowing I should try to come up with some kind of compromise, something we could both enjoy, I shut my eyes again, and this time when I opened them, the walls were light purple, the floors were dark wood, and I'd swapped the big, flashy canopy for a more normal-sized bed with a green satin headboard.

After manifesting a turquoise-colored couch that sat along the far wall, a zebra-print rug that lay right before it, a crystal chandelier that hung overhead, and a mirrored dressing table with a white velvet stool to go with it, it was time for the fun part—the accessories! So I busied myself with pillows, sheets, an aqua duvet woven with bits of silver threads, and some cool modern art that hung on the walls.

"So?" I turned to Buttercup, smiling as he put one tentative paw in front of the other, finally showing his approval in his willingness to make himself at home by sniffing every corner.

Then I gazed down at my clothes, seeing I was still wearing the same jeans, ballet flats, and T-shirt I'd had on since I'd returned from the earth plane. An outfit that just a short while before seemed super cute, but not anymore. So I closed my eyes and changed that too—swapping the jeans for skinny cargos, the ballet flats for ankle boots, and the T-shirt for a sparkly tank top and shrunken black blazer. And I was just about to manifest a new, fully loaded iPod with a zebra cover just like the rug, when the front door swung open and my parents both called, "Riley? Buttercup? You home?"

I sprang to my feet. Ready to make a mad dash for the door. Eager to see them—to see how they'd react to the makeover—until I caught a glimpse of myself in the mirror and stopped short.

The changes weren't as great as I'd thought.

They didn't really go past the surface.

The clothes just sort of hung there. And the boots made my legs look bony and ridiculous.

Replacing the old stuff with newly manifested stuff was the easy part.

The kind of real change I longed for lay just outside of my reach.

So even though I was happy to see them—no, scratch that, *overjoyed* would better describe it—instead of greeting them with the giant hug that I'd planned, I took a moment to swap the new clothes back to the old, then I stood by my couch, arms folded before me as I said, "You don't have to keep doing this, you know."

My dad stopped in the doorway, took a moment to survey the room before he looked at me and said, "Do what?" He smiled, reached toward my nose—an almost exact, albeit smaller, replica of his. Just about to tweak it in the way that always made me laugh—but right before he could, I slipped out of his grasp.

"You don't have to keep checking in on me like this! You don't have to pretend that you actually *live* here when I already know that you don't. I'm *not* a baby!" I cried, sounding, well, pretty babyish—even to my ears.

My mom stood behind him, tucking a lock of blond hair that was nearly the same color as mine back behind her ear. Her pale brow rising in a way that took all of my effort to not give into my feelings, to not let loose with the tears and barrel straight into her arms.

"Baby? Who called you a baby?" my dad asked, slipping his hands into his front pockets and shooting me a serious look.

Then before I could answer, as if on the worst kind of cue, my grandparents appeared. My grandma took one look at me and cooed, "Aw, now there's my baby girl!"

I scowled.

Like, seriously, scowled.

I mean, yeah, I was happy to see them. Yeah, I'd missed them while I was out ushering all those lost souls across the bridge. Heck, I'd even found myself mentally rehearsing the stories I'd planned to share with them later. And I fully admit that deep down inside, I even appreciated the fact that they cared enough about me to go through the charade of pretending they lived there.

Problem was, I knew better.

I knew they had other, better places to be.

I'd seen the footage. Watched the whole thing back when I was forced to go through my completely humiliating life review when I first arrived Here.

I'd seen my dad jamming with a group of musicians—rockin' out to his favorite old tunes.

I'd seen my mom in a paint-splattered smock—creating a masterpiece that back on the earth plane would've been good enough for any museum wall.

I'd seen my grandmother caring for the tiny babies that departed the earth plane too early.

I'd seen my grandfather, who'd always seemed so old and serious in all of his photos, whooping and hollering as he surfed a fifty-foot wave.

They were all enjoying their soul work—or at least that's how the Council explained it. Everyone had a job to do Here, and as much as I was beginning to enjoy mine, it was also becoming uncomfortably clear that it was all that I had.

If I wasn't out catching lost souls, I had no idea what to do with myself.

My grandmother sprang toward me, ruffled my hair in that way that she had. Wasting no time in leaving a pink-colored lipstick stain right smack on my cheek.

And when she started to go on about my being her "baby girl" yet again, my dad was quick to jump in and say, "Riley's no baby. Hasn't been for a very long time now, right, kiddo?"

Um, yeah.

Whatever.

I'd gone from *baby* to *kiddo* in just a handful of seconds. And while I guess it was progress, it really wasn't the kind of progress I was after.

All I wanted, all I ever, truly wanted, was to be thirteen.

That's. It.

And the only way I could think to achieve that was to excel at my job. To catch so many wayward ghosts that I'd end up glowing so bright the Council would have no choice but to bump up my age—along with the *physical* changes that go along with it.

And while I wasn't exactly sure that this was how it worked, it really did seem to make the most sense.

Bodhi had told me there were many levels to this place. That my pale green glow clearly marked me as a member of the level 1.5 team.

He also said that each new color got you to a new level, and that each new level was better than the one that went before. If I kept up the good work, he assured me I'd be transcending that level and color in no time.

And there was no doubt I was transcending. Since my time in the Caribbean, my glow had grown even deeper.

But now, thanks to the Council, I had no immediate ghosts to cross over.

No way to glow myself into being a teenager.

This forced vacation was holding me back.

"You know, I think you're right!" my grandma said, exchanging a quick look with my dad—one they'd convinced themselves that I'd missed. "Riley's no baby at all! And would you look at that glow!"

She was placating me. There was no getting around it.

But she also loved me, wanted the best for me. There was no getting around that either.

So I folded. Heaved a big, loud sigh and sank right down onto my turquoise-colored couch, where I leaned back against the cushions and clutched a purple satin pillow flat against my (completely flat) chest. Watching as my mom, my dad, my grandpa, and grandma busied themselves with admiring all the changes I'd made in my room.

They examined the color of the walls, tested the bounce and firmness of my bed, ran their hands over my silk head-board, my dressing table, the silver picture frames that punctuated the walls—all the while exclaiming how grown-up and sophisticated it looked. Correctly assuming those were the buzzwords, they were quick to repeat them again and again.

I watched them in action. Watched with a big, solid lump lodged right in my throat. And when my grandma sat beside me and placed her hand on my knee, when my grandpa sat cross-legged on the floor with Buttercup right at his feet, when my mom and dad both perched on the edge of my bed—I continued to watch. Taking in the varying shades of pale skin, blond hair, and blue eyes they all shared, and realizing it was like looking at old, and really old versions of myself.

We were family.

Alive, dead, it didn't make the least bit of difference.

Wherever we might go from here, wherever we might end up, there was no doubt we'd always hold traces of each other.

I was never as alone as I'd thought.

They looked at me, eyes expectant, my grandpa taking the lead and speaking for all of them when he said, "So, tell us where you've been, already! Tell us how you got that glow of yours!"

And because I loved them—because I knew they loved me—I did.

5

My grandpa taught me to surf. My mom helped me to paint a somewhat decent landscape. My grandma showed me how to swaddle a newborn in its blanket, while my dad showed great patience when he let me sing lead in his band. And as much fun as I had, after a while, there was no doubt it was time to move on.

While none of them actually said as much, it was clear I couldn't carry on like that forever. It was time to strike out on my own. Build some kind of life outside of Soul Catching and family. Maybe even make a few friends.

So I set out to do just that, with Buttercup right there beside me. My direction clear, my intentions pure, everything looking so bright and upbeat, so full of promise—or at least that's how I felt right up until the moment I saw them.

Even though I have a history of spying on everyone from my sister, Ever, back when I was alive—to A-list celebrities after I was dead—to the former teachers, neighbors, and friends I sometimes checked in on from the Viewing Room— on that particular day, spying was the furthest thing from my mind.

On that particular day, I was really and truly just minding my own business as though all thoughts of Bodhi and Jasmine had been erased from my brain.

But the second I stumbled upon them—the second I saw the way they acted when they thought no one was looking—well, even though I knew I should've moved on, I found that I no longer could.

My legs went all clumsy and heavy. My limbs froze in place. And all I could do was just stand there and gape, knowing I should go before one of them saw me.

Only they didn't see me.

They were too busy looking at each other.

Bodhi sprawled across the grass, his back propped against a thick tree trunk, his legs thrust out before him, while Jasmine curled up beside him, her head on his knees.

He read from a big book of poetry, employing long, thoughtful pauses to allow the words to sink in. One hand grasping the book, the other smoothing her long, dark braids, causing the glass beads to chime and swish in a soft, lilting melody—causing her lips to curve, her face to glow, and her eyes to grow all sparkly and dreamy.

Like a scene from a movie—the kind Ever and her friends used to watch.

The kind that just a few years before would've made me go: *blech!* and: *gag!* And make an entire soundtrack of gross-out sounds to go with it.

But not anymore.

Watching them together like that . . . well, it gave me that weird, hollow feeling again.

It made me feel so quiet and wistful—I suddenly knew what it meant to feel melancholy.

And when Bodhi lifted his hand, flattened his palm, and manifested a beautiful flower he then tucked behind her ear—a jasmine for Jasmine—well, I couldn't stop watching— even when the sight of it made my insides start to swirl.

This was not the Bodhi I knew.

This was not the straw-munching, semi-pro skater dude who really liked to argue—or at least he really liked to argue with me.

Things were different with Jasmine.

It was the exact opposite of the way he acted with me.

It was the exact opposite of the way anyone would *ever* act with me as long as I was stuck as a shrimpy, skinny, flat-chested twelve-year-old kid.

As long as I remained in that state, no boy would ever read me poetry.

No boy would ever tuck a flower into my hair.

And suddenly a thought that I wouldn't have even cared about just six months before had me so freaked my whole body trembled, causing Buttercup to tune in to my mood, toss back his head, and let out a long, mournful howl.

"Buttercup—shush!" I'd whispered, but it was too late. Jasmine had already spotted me, and it wasn't long before Bodhi looked up and saw me as well—shouting my name with a voice that rang of shock and surprise, with more than a hint of anger tossed in.

But instead of responding, I ran—dragging a reluctant Buttercup along with me.

We ran from the clearing.

Ran past streams that turned into rivers, and rivers that turned into lakes. We ran right out of the forest of trees and wide-open spaces, and into a city filled with tall crystal buildings.

We ran until we both grew too pooped to continue.

We ran until we remembered it was so much easier to fly.

I soared as high as I could, and then higher still. Buttercup gliding alongside me, his ears flapping like crazy, his mouth stretched and curled as though he was grinning. But while my dog was enjoying the flight—my only goal was to flee. My head was spinning, my insides thrumming, and I wanted nothing more than to erase what I'd seen.

Wanted nothing more than to rid myself of the horrible, desperate feeling it had stirred up inside me.

And even though I wasn't supposed to do it, even though I'd been told it was strictly forbidden, even though I'd already gotten in trouble for it on more than one occasion, that wasn't enough to keep me from stopping by the Viewing Room.

I needed to see my sister, Ever. Needed to find a way to be with her, communicate with her. Thinking that doing so might make me feel better.

Remembering what the Council had told me:

Take some time off.

Spend time with family. Visit with friends.

Using it as just the excuse that I needed to stop before the door, and push my way in.

6

The second I saw that purple-and-orange Hawaiian shirt (the exact same one he was wearing the last time I saw him, but who was I to judge?) along with the plaid Bermuda shorts, the black dress socks, and the shiny black shoes—well, I knew for sure it was fate.

Destiny.

There was no doubt in my mind it was kismet.

Meant to be.

Why else would Mort, the guy who started all this, the guy who first told me about the place where all the dreams happen—why else would I find him standing right in front of me?

For the second time in a row, even?

And just when I was wondering if he'd recognize me, he turned and smiled and said, "Heya, newbie!"

Newbie?

I squinted. Not quite sure how to take that. Thinking at first he was taking a swipe at my age, but it wasn't long before I realized he was referring to my glow.

I was green. He was yellow. So clearly he'd been Here longer. You could tell just by looking.

I smiled in return. Furtively looking over his shoulder for the friend he'd been with the last time I'd seen him—the one who was reluctant to share much of anything. And, as fate would have it, he wasn't there—something I took as another good sign.

"So, you find it?" Mort asked, taking his place at the front of the line when a cubicle was vacated and the person before him went in.

I shook my head, careful to keep my voice lower than usual when I said, "Or at least not yet, anyway."

Mort looked me over, his two bushy brows merging together until they looked like an overfed caterpillar had collapsed on his forehead.

"Do you think you could help? Or maybe even show me where it is? I mean, I know you're busy and all, and I'm willing to wait. I was just hoping that maybe—"

But before I could finish, another stall was vacated and a loud voice called, "Next!"

Mort's hands grew antsy, curling and uncurling by his

sides, clearly eager to get inside the cubicle, observe his old life.

And knowing I had only a handful of seconds before I lost him completely, I said, "I-just-thought-you-could-maybe-point-me-in-the-right-direction?" The words coming so quickly, they all blurred as one.

He wavered, glancing between the cubicle and me. And just when I was sure that I'd lost him, that he'd decided against me, he sighed, waved in the person behind him, and said, "Guess you got an important message to share, eh?"

I nodded. Even though I had no idea what that message might be, I knew that if I wanted his help, if I wanted to get to the place where the dreams go to happen, it was better to keep that fact to myself.

He screwed his mouth to the side, causing his cheek to stretch and the wrinkles to flatten and fade. Returning to normal again when his lips dropped back into place, and he said, "I've got a granddaughter your age—name's Daisy. What're you—ten?"

I groaned. Like, seriously groaned. I didn't even try to stifle it. He'd insulted me in the very worst way.

But Mort just laughed. Laughed for so long I was more than ready to cut my losses and strike out on my own, when he finally sobered up enough to say, "You sure you want to do this?"

I thought about my sister and how much I missed her.

I thought about seeing Bodhi with Jasmine and the way it made me feel.

And when my eyes met Mort's, well that's when I knew that Bodhi had lied. The place where all the dreams happen wasn't forbidden—Bodhi was just doing his best to kill all my fun.

"Yeah, I'd really like to visit," I said, my voice deep and serious. "Will you help me find it?"

Mort glanced around the Viewing Room, rubbed his chin with a surprisingly well-manicured hand, then a moment later, he headed for the door. Holding it open and motioning for me to go through as he said, "After you, then."

7

As it turned out, Mort wasn't nearly as charmed with the concept of flying as Buttercup and I were.

Mort was old-school.

Other than the occasional trip to the Viewing Room and the area where the dreams all take place, it seemed he worked pretty hard to keep to a life that was very similar to the one he'd lived back on the earth plane. And since he was the only one I knew who could help me to get there, I had no choice but to do it his way. Which pretty much meant that we hitched a ride on the train.

We settled onto our seats, Buttercup and me on one side, Mort on the other, and we'd only gone a bit down the tracks when he started telling me all about Daisy, his grand-daughter.

I nodded. Smiled. Listened as intently as I could, making sure to laugh in all the right places. And even though she sounded really nice and sweet, like someone I might like to know if it wasn't too late—if I wasn't already dead—I still have to say that, for the record, she didn't sound the slightest bit like me.

For starters, the music she liked, well, it was kind of embarrassing.

And don't even get me started on her favorite TV shows and movies.

Still, it was clear that Mort missed her. And because of it, because I was somewhat close to her age, he was determined to find a connection that, to be honest, just wasn't there.

"So, do you ever visit her in her dreams?" I asked, trying to stay somewhat on topic, while steering it in a direction that was much closer to my own interests.

He nodded, mumbling, "All the time," as he gazed out the window. Eyes narrowing as though he could actually make out the scenery, even though whenever I looked all I could get was a fuzzy, gray blur. "Kids are very receptive to that sort of thing," he said. "And Daisy's no different. When she was younger, just a baby, I used to skip the dreams altogether and pop in for a visit instead. I used to sing to her, read her stories in her crib—we had ourselves a great time." He laughed, gaze far away as though viewing it again in his head. "And then later, when she could talk, she used to tell her mom—my daughter Delilah—she used to tell her that Grampy had just stopped by. That's what she called me, Grampy. Though of course her mom didn't believe her. Adults never do." He shook his head. "They're too skeptical. Too close-minded. Think they've got it all figured out—that they know all there is. Heck, I was the same way . . . or at least I was until I found myself Here." He laughed again and looked away.

"So, you're allowed to do that? Drop in for an actual visit, I mean?" I frowned, that was certainly news to me. So far my only visits had been for Soul Catching, and a vacation that turned into Soul Catching. I didn't think we could just drop in whenever we pleased.

But Mort, sensing my growing excitement, was quick to correct me. His expression gone suddenly careful, guarded, he said, "Now don't go getting any ideas." He shot me a stern look. "That was all a while ago. Way back before I knew any better. While nothing's exactly forbidden per se . . . well, that kind of thing, those earth plane visits, they're not exactly encouraged either. Besides, all it usually amounts to is a big waste of time. Other than dogs and little kids, most people can't see us."

He went on and on, but I was no longer listening. I was still stuck on the part when he said nothing was forbidden.

Was it true?

Could it possibly be?

And if so, does that mean Bodhi had lied to me?

"See, the thing is," Mort continued, his voice pitching louder, invading my thoughts. "They don't want us interfering too much. Each soul, each person, has to find their own way—learn their own lessons. And let's face it, most people only learn the hard way. No one ever volunteers for change. Even when the situation they're in makes them unhappy, most people would rather stick with the unhappy they know, than take a chance on something unknown. And I'll tell ya from experience that it's not an easy thing to watch. But, in the end, it's all for the best. It's all those rough bits that make us stronger. The tough stuff makes us grow and mature. Which is why you can't go around protecting everyone from the world that they live in. You have to let them learn to navigate it all on their own. If you interfere, if you don't let them find their own way, you'll stunt them, keep them from learning, progressing. And I'll tell you right now, that sort of thing leads to no good."

I nodded as though I understood every word, as though I agreed wholeheartedly. Though, the truth is, my gaze was unsteady, unfocused, as a blur of thoughts and images swirled through my head.

"And, as you'll soon see, they're very careful to regulate that sort of well-intentioned interference when it comes to dream visitations. Though there are ways to get around it, the truth is, it's rarely worth the bother. It requires loads of complicated symbolism, and for the most part, people either can't remember it, or worse, they muck it all up when they try to interpret it. I gave all that up a while ago. It just got too frustrating. Now I just pop in when I can, try to send a little comfort and love, and leave it at that."

"And does it work?" I asked, remembering what I overheard Mort saying to his friend the first time I saw them. How he often visited his grieving wife in her dreams, wanting her to know he was A-okay. But the moment she woke up, she shrugged it off—convinced herself it wasn't real. Just something her brain cooked up to make her feel good.

I looked at him, waiting for an answer, but then the train came to a halt, the doors sprang wide open, and Mort looked at me and said, "This is it. Dreamland. We're here."

8

It probably doesn't make much sense to say: "It's not what I thought it would be," about a place you never really thought about before. And yet, those were the first words that sprang to mind when I gazed upon the big, sparkly, half moon–shaped sign that read: WELCOME TO DREAMLAND.

It wasn't at all like I'd thought.

I guess I was expecting it to be more like a movie theater. A big dark room full of chairs with cup holders punched into the arms, and a large, wide screen projecting all kinds of crazy, mixed-up images that somehow found their way to the dreamer.

But instead, I was greeted by a tall iron gate and a glass-enclosed guardhouse with a very serious-looking guard who studied us closely.

Mort made his way forward, said a quick and friendly hello, then patiently waited, thumbs hitched into his belt loops, humming an unfamiliar tune, as the guard gave him a thorough once-over. Tapping the tip of his pointy red pen along the edge of a long sheet of paper until he found what he was looking for, placed a thick check mark beside it, then shot Mort another stern look as he waved him right in. And even though Buttercup and I were quick on Mort's heels, hoping to sneak in alongside him, it seems Buttercup was quicker than I was.

The second my foot tried to sneak its way in, the gate slammed closed before me, as the guard glared and said, "State your name and your business, please."

I gulped, gazed longingly at my friends who were standing where I needed to be, mumbling a quick: "Uh, my name is Riley Bloom." Trying my best not to fiddle with my fingers, chew my hair, twitch my knee, or engage in any other kind of nervous giveaway as I watched him flick his pen down the long sheet of paper. "As for my business . . ." I arranged my face into what I hoped resembled a pleasant smile, thinking a little friendliness might help speed things along. "Well, I'm hoping to send someone a dream."

Mort gasped, wheezed, cleared his throat in a way that was so much louder than necessary. And when my eyes found his, I knew just what he was up to—he was trying to divert the attention from me.

Although it may have seemed as though I hadn't really

said much of anything, apparently what I had said was enough to keep me from entering.

But it was too late. The guard had already narrowed his eyes, was already in the middle of saying, "Excuse me? What did you just say?"

He leaned forward, pressing toward me in a way that, well, had I still been alive would've made me blush crimson. Though, as it was, I just stood there all bug-eyed and mute, replaying my words, unable to pinpoint just where I'd failed.

I glanced at Mort, hoping he could help, but from the resigned look in his eyes, I was all on my own.

"Um, what I meant was that I'm here to send someone a dream." Already cringing well before the words were all out. Seeing the guard's mouth go all twisty and grim, as Mort just sighed and covered his face with his hands. "I mean, maybe I'm not familiar with the lingo, maybe I don't know all the correct terms, but all I want to do is . . ."

Dream visitation. Tell him you're here for a dream visitation!

Although it seemed like the thought just randomly popped into my head, I knew there was nothing random about it. Not even close. The words came with Mort's unmistakable East Coast accent. It wasn't so much a telepathic message, as an order I'd better seriously follow if I wanted to be on the same side of the gate as Buttercup and him.

a l y s o n   n o ë l

"I just want to, uh, visit someone in a dream," I said, holding the smile that was growing so stiff it made my cheeks sting. "You know, like a dream visitation, that's all."

The guard looked at me, his face still stern. Holding his silence for so long, I was just about to cut my losses and leave, when he said, "So why didn't you say so?" He shook his head, scribbled my name at the bottom of his list before placing a fat red check mark beside it. "And just so you know, for the record, we don't *create* dreams here, young lady. *Dreamweaving* hasn't taken place for . . ." He frowned, gazed into the distance as though studying an invisible calendar only he could see. "Well . . . let's just say it's no longer done. Though, if you're interested in a *dream jump,* well, then you've come to the right place." He smiled brightly, his eyes shining, his cheeks widening—the change so dramatic, so startling, he looked like an entirely different person. "Only a few hours 'til closing though. Not sure if they'll get to you today. But just in case, you better wear this."

He slid me a badge that I immediately attached to my tee. The gate opened before me as I wondered how a place like this could actually close, when back home on the earth plane, people were dreaming in all different time zones. Loads of people heading for sleep just as a whole other load were starting their day. But knowing better than to push it,

60

I decided to just shrug and smile and add it to the long list of things that didn't make any sense.

No sooner was I safely inside, when a heavily accented voice said, "*Gah!* Who *is* this wonder? What is this vision I see here before me?"

I turned toward the voice, curious to see whom it belonged to. Noticing the way Mort stepped quickly aside, his face full of awe, as he made way for a short, rotund man with a wispy goatee and dark glossy hair that appeared solid black, aside from the thick white skunk stripe that fell down the front.

The man strode closer, the legs of his stretchy riding pants rubbing ominously together, as his knee-high boots smacked hard against the concrete in a chorus of doom. I narrowed my gaze on his tight blue shirt, noting how the buttons were *this* close to popping, while his silk, paisley scarf twisted loosely around his neck, once, twice, before floating behind him like a swirl of hazy jetstream.

And the next thing I knew, he was standing before us, hand clutched to his chest as he said, "Aw, but she is *perfetto*! Perfection—I say! Hurry now, *vite-vite*—there is no time to waste!"

I paused, looking to Mort for guidance, unsure what to do. After the ordeal with the guard I was afraid of saying or doing anything wrong.

But a second later, the strange little man was tugging on my sleeve, pulling me toward him as he said, "You must come—and quickly! She is just what I have asked for! A gift that has arrived—how do you say? In the very nick of time! How did you know that I needed you now?" He glanced my way, eyebrow arched high, not allowing any time to reply before he waved his hand before him and said, "Never mind! I do not question the how—I accept this gift as it is. There is no time to waste—no time at all! Just, please, this must be worn—" He thrust a pair of pristine white gossamer wings into my arms. "Now, quickly, you must follow, vite-vite! We must not delay!"

I rushed alongside him, bolted over a wide swath of concrete, over a winding trail of grass, followed by a path of crumbly asphalt. Going right past a big, surprisingly run-down, abandoned building, slowing my pace as I struggled to get the wings securely placed on my back. Having no idea what they might be for, but so happy to be moving away from the gate I decided not to ask.

"I thought it was over. I was sure I would be forced to compromise—something of which I, Balthazar, am not fond, not fond at all." He glanced at Buttercup, smiling brightly as he added, "A dream is a delicate recipe—consisting of only the purest ingredients. A dream must be handled with great care. Like soufflé!" He clapped his hands together, delighted with his own metaphor. "A delicate balance with no room for substitutes. I was all out of options, I was *this* close to leaving—" He pinched his thumb and forefinger together, held it high over his shoulder so that Buttercup, Mort, and I could all see. "I think to myself: *Balthazar, maybe this time you really do quit. Maybe now is when you retire for good!* And then, the very next moment, what do I see?"

He stopped so abruptly I nearly crashed into his side, and it took a moment to realize he was actually awaiting a reply.

I smiled serenely, using the *Mona Lisa* as my guide. My chin lowered, eyes downcast, voice quiet and humbled as I said, "I am honored to be of service. I do have a very strange knack for showing up at just the right time."

I paused, swaddled in the comfort of feeling rather pleased with myself. Then I lifted my eyes to meet his, and that's when I realized it wasn't exactly *me* that he found so *magnifico* and *perfetto*.

Nope, it wasn't me at all.

It was Buttercup that had him enthralled.

Balthazar squinted as though seeing me for the very first time, which, I soon realized, he was.

"What is this?" He scoffed, face creased into a scowl as he yanked away the wings he'd thrust at me earlier. "You make joke with me? Is that it? Balthazar has great sense of humor, everyone agrees. But now is not time for jokes! Balthazar has very important work! The dreamer will awaken if we do not move quickly—all will be lost!" He shook his head, muttered under his breath, and struggled to place the wings onto a very unhappy, not-so-cooperative Buttercup.

Still feeling a little annoyed by the way I'd been treated, the way I'd come in second place to my dog, I placed my hands on my hips and said, "Um, okay, but just so you know, Buttercup is a he, *not* a she. Also, he doesn't need wings to fly, he can manage just fine on his own."

Balthazar's eyes grew wide, and then wider still. Hardly able to believe his good fortune as he grabbed hold of Buttercup's collar and ran, leaving Mort and me to struggle to catch up with them.

"Balthazar has an artistic temperament," Mort told me, his words punctuated by the sound of his black dress shoes pounding the asphalt. "He can get a bit . . . *testy* at times, but that's only because he's such a perfectionist. He has vision. Remarkable vision. He's a master. The absolute best. No one can handle a dream jump like him. He's just as big a legend Here as he was on the earth plane. Not to worry, Buttercup is in good hands."

"But who *is* Balthazar?" I asked, choosing to slow, no

longer trying to keep up their pace. Mort shot me a strange look then pointed at the fading figure ahead, but I just shook my head and said, "No, what I meant was, *who* is he? What does he *do* here?"

Mort turned, brows quirked in disbelief. "Balthazar runs the place! Has for years. Back when he was alive, he was one of the most celebrated directors of all time. Got a shelf full of Oscars to prove it. Now that he's Here he oversees all the dream jumps. Has a handful of assistant directors to help him, but make no mistake, he's in charge. You got a dream visitation in mind, you gotta go through him. He's your only hope. He decides who makes the cut."

9

"She is a natural. She has done this before, no?"

I gazed down the tip of Balthazar's pointing finger, watching Buttercup take flight, soaring back and forth across a set arranged to look like a beautiful enchanted garden—complete with blooming trees, a sparkling lawn, and a glistening lake populated by a small group of black and white swans.

"*He*," I said, my voice more than a little testy, maybe too testy. But still, how many times would I be forced to say it before he understood? "Buttercup is a *he*," I repeated, but it was no use, my words fell on deaf ears. Balthazar merely waved it away, jumped from his chair, and motioned for Buttercup to soar higher, for the swans to glide faster, as a guy who looked to be in his twenties walked hand in hand with a girl, whispering softly into her ear.

I hoisted myself onto the director's chair an assistant

had brought me, crossing one leg over the other, and turning to Mort, just about to ask him a question when he shook his head and pointed toward the sign overhead with the bright red letters that read: SILENCE! DREAM IN PROGRESS!

Left with no choice but to shelve all my questions 'til later, I took a good look around, taking in the hive of activity, the sheer amount of work it took to make a dream happen. It was surprising to say the least.

Up until then I'd always assumed that dreams were . . . well . . . a whole lot simpler than what I saw unfolding before me. I always assumed they were woven from remnants of random thoughts and experiences that happened during the day—bits and pieces of things seen and heard, mixed in with mere figments of the imagination. All of it sort of swirling together like some kind of fantastical, subconscious soup. Or at least that was the gist of the dream interpretation book Ever got me one year for Christmas. But according to what I saw happening in Dreamland, that book was dead wrong.

It was a production.

Like a major, big-time production.

Reminding me of the time my class took a field trip to see an opera in Portland, not long before I died.

Just like the opera, the set was elaborate, carefully crafted, containing a whole crew of actors, including my dog, who continued to fly overhead. Yet there was also a whole crew of people working off the stage too. Including costume designers, makeup artists, and hair stylists, as well as lighting technicians, a stunt person or two, and a whole team that, from what I could see, were in charge of the special effects.

Also like the opera, there was a pit at the edge of the stage where the orchestra sat. A small group of musicians clutching a strange variety of horns, and cans, and chains, and, yeah, some even had the kind of musical instruments you might expect—all of them keeping a close eye on Balthazar— awaiting their signal, to make just the right sound, at just the right moment.

It was amazing.

Absolutely and completely amazing.

Watching it all unfold right before me, well, I couldn't help but take a quick mental inventory of all the old dreams I remembered from my past, unable to see them the same way I once had.

Though unlike the opera, it seemed it was over before it could really get started. And the next thing I knew Balthazar leaped from his chair and shouted, "She's awake! That's a wrap! Good work, everyone!"

The girl vanished—like, one second she was there and the next, *not*. And while the crew busied themselves with clearing the stage and dismantling the set, the guy wiped the tears from his eyes and profusely thanked Balthazar—telling him that for the first time since his death, he felt like he'd truly gotten through to his grieving fiancée.

Buttercup bounded toward the pile of doggy biscuits Balthazar held in his hand. All puffed up and self-satisfied with his performance, his newfound star power, he went about the business of busily wolfing them down, as Balthazar smiled and said, "Here he is—the true star of this show!" Then looking at me, he added, "I am in your debt. Because of your dog, the dream was saved. The girl was dreaming of a beautiful field of sparkling lakes, black and white swans, and, believe it or not, angelic, flying dogs. And, as I had none on hand, when you showed up when you did—well, it saved the entire production. So please, tell me, how can I ever repay you?"

I pressed my lips together, struggled to make sense of his words. What he'd just said was entirely different from what I thought I'd just witnessed.

"Wait—" I squinted, shook my head. "You mean to say that you didn't actually *create* that dream?" I gazed right at him, noting how he was so short, he was exactly eye level with me. "Are you saying that you merely *re-created* a dream that was *already in progress*?" My mind ran with the concept—it was an even bigger feat than I'd imagined.

I glanced toward Mort, alerted by the way his eyebrows

shot up so high they practically blended into his scalp, and when my gaze landed on Balthazar again, well, he just looked at me and balked.

Like, seriously balked.

His lips flattening, whitening, as his nostrils flared, his ears twitched, and his cheeks threatened to explode in a burst of red, anger-fueled fury.

And then, just when I was sure it couldn't get any worse, I watched, completely mortified (completely mystified!), as Balthazar spun on his heel and stormed away without another word.

10

For someone who had just professed to be in my debt—
for someone who had just claimed that because of my
dog I had heroically saved the day—for someone who
claimed to have ginormous gobs of gratitude reserved just
for me—well, all I can say is that when Balthazar stormed
away, it pretty much cancelled all that.

Buttercup slunk to his belly and let out a low, sorrowful
whimper, as Mort mumbled a whole string of words under
his breath that sounded like, *"Oh boy, now you've done it . . ."*
I just stood there and gaped, having no idea what I'd done to
offend Balthazar in such a big, apparently unforgivable way.

It was Mort who finally went after him, somehow convincing him to stop long enough to hear him out. And though
I still have no idea what he said, I do know that Balthazar
reconsidered, turned, and finally made his way back where
he stood before me, taking great care to enunciate each and

every word as he said, "I am told this is your first visit to Dreamland, no?"

I nodded, far too afraid to say something wrong.

He paused, studied me closely, fingering the knotted silk scarf at his throat. "And so, this . . . this . . . *ignorance* of yours, it must be forgiven, yes?"

I nodded again. Not really liking the word "ignorance" being so easily applied to me, but knowing better than to say anything.

"And so, we shall agree to never speak of it again?"

I glanced between Mort and Buttercup, saw their dual nods of encouragement. Then I looked at Balthazar, and said, "Um, okay . . . I just thought maybe you could help me send a dream to my sister, but I guess I misunderstood, so . . ."

Mort gasped.

Buttercup placed his paws over his eyes.

And just when I was sure it couldn't get any worse, Balthazar spoke in a voice that was quite a bit higher, quite a bit screechier than I'd come to expect. "Correction!" he practically shouted. "We do not *send* dreams. Nor do we *create* dreams, but, rather, we *dream jump*. You would like to *dream jump*, I think, yes?"

He nodded. Nodded in a way that told me that if I knew what was good for me then I would nod too.

So I did.

And then, I cleared my throat and said, *"Yes,"* just to reiterate.

And then I nodded again.

It may have been overkill. But heck, practically from the moment I'd arrived I'd said everything wrong. From what I could tell, these people were really stuck on using just the right words, so I don't think I can be blamed for trying to do something right for a change.

Though luckily, it seemed to work, because Balthazar just looked at me and said, "Good. Now, please, come with me, Miss Riley Bloom."

According to Balthazar, time, or rather, the time of day, really wasn't all that important where dream jumping was concerned. Something which I considered a good thing, since A: from what I'd been told, there is no time in the Here & Now, and B: also from what I'd been told, Dreamland had some pretty strict opening and closing hours.

Also according to Balthazar, a person didn't have to be asleep to receive a message. While it may be the preferred way—mostly because the dream state lowers a person's defenses, leaving them more receptive to messages from the beyond—it wasn't entirely necessary. It wasn't the only way.

Apparently a message could be sent just as easily when a person drifted off in a daydream (something that I used to do a lot of in my math class) or even, surprisingly enough, while going for a very long drive.

"Driving is meditative," he said. "A lot of people—how do you say?" He paused, finger placed on his chin, taking a moment to capture the word he was hunting. "A lot of people *zone out* when they drive." He looked at me, nodding, skunk hair wagging before a pair of darkly twinkling eyes.

I couldn't help but giggle at the way he'd sounded when he said *zone out*. *Perfetto* and *magnifico* were two words I'd already grown used to—they were words that suited his strange, quasi-European accent. But hearing that same accent pronounce *zone out* . . . well, it was just so hilarious I couldn't resist the laugh that burst out.

"And, if that is not possible," he added, ignoring the way I bent forward, clutched at my belly. "There is always music."

I looked at him. He had my full attention again.

"Music is one of the highest art forms there is. It can define a life, change a life, or even save a life, in just three short minutes. It's got a direct link to the divine. All art forms do, of course, but music . . ." His gaze went all bleary as he stared off into the distance, searching for a better way to explain it, but then he shook his head, waved his hand before him, and said, "Anyway . . . so tell me, have you ever heard just the right song at just the right moment?"

I pressed my lips together as I thought long and hard—pretty sure that I had. No, on second thought, I most definitely had. More than once for that matter.

He nodded, having already assumed the answer. "That was someone trying to send you a message."

My jaw dropped, my tongue went all lumpy and speechless, and I remembered all the times in the past when I'd been either scared, or nervous, or sad, or all three, and how the song my mom always used to play for me when I was baby, a song by James Taylor, the same song her parents played for her, would just magically appear on the radio, or play on TV, or sometimes even a car would go by that had it blasting from its stereo.

My comfort song.

Or at least that's how I used to think of it. And yet, every time that happened, on every single one of those occasions, I'd written it off as some sort of crazy coincidence.

But suddenly I knew better.

I finally knew the truth.

Contrary to what most people think, coincidences are few and far between.

"And then, of course, there is also the thoughtwave." He

waved his hand dismissively and wrinkled his nose, his face displaying such distaste I couldn't help but wonder why he even chose to mention it in the first place. Then before I could ask for more details, he said, "A thoughtwave can be done by anyone. There is no training required. It is where the sender simply finds a quiet place and concentrates very hard with a particular message that may, or may not, reach the receiver. It is simple. Sometimes effective, sometimes not, depends. But to my taste . . ." He ran his hand over his chin, tugged lightly on his goatee, his thumb sporting a nail that was twice as long as mine. "Well . . . let's just say that it is *not* to my taste. So, to conclude, while there are many ways to send a message, still, whenever possible, dream jumping is the preferred method. When done right, the sender, as well as the receiver, are able to share something that is both special and unique."

"And when done wrong?" I had no idea why I said it. I guess the words just popped out before I could stop them.

But luckily, Balthazar just laughed. His head shaking, his goatee twitching, when he said, "I would not know about this. We never do it wrong around here. I insist it is done right or it is not done at all. And so, what do you think? Are you ready to begin?"

II

While Mort was prepping for his own dream jump, Buttercup and I were in Balthazar's office—a small space consisting of a couch, two chairs, and a desk. Its walls covered with posters of some, if not all, the old movies I assumed Balthazar had directed back in his Hollywood days, and believe me, there were a lot of them.

I settled onto a chair as Buttercup sniffed his way around, needing to investigate every corner, sometimes more than once, before he'd settle down. Balthazar slipped on a pair of sparkly red reading glasses, settled back onto his worn leather chair, grabbed a notepad and a pen, and set about the business of grilling me with all kinds of questions about my past—or, as he called it: my *backstory*.

Basically, he wanted to know as much as I could (or in my case, as much as I *would*) tell him about my relationship with the receiver.

That's what he called her, my sister, Ever, the receiver—whereas I was known as the sender.

Or, at least, I hoped to be. He still hadn't said for sure if he'd let me proceed. Apparently it all depended on the backstory.

If he found my story compelling, my motivation convincing—if he deemed it worthy of everyone's time, he'd teach me to dream jump.

But if not, well . . . I preferred not to think about that.

I guess there was a very long list of people waiting for a chance to work with him, but because of Buttercup's showing up at just the right time and saving the dream jump in progress, he was willing to do me a favor by letting me skip to the front of the line. But whether or not I'd get any further depended on his being intrigued by my backstory.

So, I dove in. Telling him all about me, and my family, how we died in a car accident—including how I stuck around the earth plane long after that so I could continue to visit (or *haunt*, depending on how you chose to look at it) my big sister, Ever. Going into as much detail as I could, taking great care to keep it entertaining, to keep it from getting too factual, too boring. I had a feeling he was the type to bore easily—that while he may have insisted on hearing the motivation, he had no interest in the day-to-day details. Trips to the dentist, the first time I made my own sandwich—those were the sort of things I kept to myself. And every time he started to fool with his goatee, twirling it between his fore-finger and thumb, I knew I'd better speed things up, or lose him completely.

But when it came time to reveal just what kind of mes-sage I wanted to send . . . well, that's when the whole thing fell apart.

I stuttered.

Spluttered.

The words lodged in my throat until I completely stalled out.

Completely embarrassed by how bad I'd flubbed up—and yet, I would've been far more embarrassed to admit that my message wasn't so much to help Ever, as it was to help myself.

I mean, yeah, I wanted her to know that I loved her and missed her and all that. I also wanted to share some of my worries about the kind of life she'd found herself in—and my real and valid concerns that I might never get to see her again. Though I wasn't exactly willing to share any of that with Balthazar, so it just became more information I kept to myself.

Still, if I'm going to be 100 percent honest, then I'll have to admit that the dream jump was mostly for me.

I needed reassurance.

I needed some good and solid advice.

I needed Ever to tell me how to make friends—how to get teenagers to like me.

How to get boys to take notice of me.

The kinds of things I'd never even thought about, much less worried about, before.

But mostly, I needed her to tell me how to be a teen. It was all I ever really wanted—and yet, I had no idea how to proceed.

If the Council was going to force me to take a break from Soul Catching—the only way I knew how to increase my glow, which in turn might make me grow and mature—then I had no choice but to seek advice from the most amazing teenager I knew—Ever, my sister.

And though I wasn't actually dumb enough to think one visit with her would make me thirteen—I was pretty convinced that if I could just learn how to *act* it, then someday, hopefully soon, I could *be* it.

But when my eyes met Balthazar's, well, I knew I couldn't share any of that—not when I could barely admit it to myself.

So instead, I encouraged him to fill up his notebook with a random, but carefully chosen assortment of somewhat relevant facts. And when it came time for more, well, I just lifted my shoulders, lowered my eyes, and told him that

I had no agenda. Told him my only goal was to check in, see how it flowed, and take it from there.

His pen crashed to his desk. He leaned all the way back in his chair and leveled his eyes right on mine. And even though I didn't have a lot of interview experience to go on, I was pretty sure Balthazar's body language signaled a fail.

Which is why I couldn't have been more surprised when he said, *"Perfetto!"*

I looked at him. Blinked. Wondered if I'd misunderstood.

"Magnifico!" He clapped his hands together, once, twice, before he rested them against the outward curve of his belly. "This is so *pure*! So . . . *honest*!" He swung his chair forward, gripped the sides of his desk. "We will let the story flow . . . we will keep it natural, organic. This is truly *fantastico*! I cannot wait to get started!" His eyebrows jumped as his goatee twitched back and forth.

Then he leaped from his seat, skirted his desk, and yanked hard on my sleeve, pulling me through a side door I'd failed to notice before. Whisking Buttercup and me along a series of halls, before he stopped, pressed a short, stubby finger to his chin, and said, "Here is where we begin."

I followed him inside, amazed to find the kind of space I'd originally envisioned—a small, dark theater with chairs, a projector, and a screen.

Buttercup settled at my feet as Balthazar claimed the seat right beside me. Crossing his legs, he folded his hands onto his knees, his voice low and serious when he said, "We begin as we always begin—in silence. You will close your eyes. You will go very, very quiet—very, very deep. You will remember your sister. You will make a mental picture of her to fill up your head. Then, when the picture is complete, you will tune in to her energy pattern. Like fingerprints, everyone has one. And, also like fingerprints, each one is unique. Then, while you are busy with that, I will take this energy's . . . how do you say . . ." He looked at me, squinted, but I just lifted my shoulders in reply, I had no idea where he was headed. "I will take this energy's *imprint*." He nodded. "Yes, that's it. *Imprint*. The imprint is the most important thing. Without it, we can do nothing. Understand?"

Honestly? I didn't. I didn't understand a single thing he'd said. None of it made the least bit of sense. But, the way he looked at me, his eyes wide, head bobbing, I knew I was expected to widen my eyes and bob my head too.

So I did.

And then I closed my eyes and tried to appear as though I was following all the other directions as well. Picturing my sister, zooming in on her image until she filled up my head. Trying to tune in to her energy, her *imprint,* even though I really had no idea what that meant.

Mostly I just sat there and thought about her. Remembering the way she looked—a lot like me with the blond hair and blue eyes—though unlike me in that her nose was *not* semi-stubby—her chest was *not* sadly sunken. Ever was pretty and popular in the way I could only hope to be.

I remembered how she laughed—the sound sort of light, tinkly, and girly. Then I remembered how she laughed a lot less after surviving the accident—and just how hard I had to work to kick-start her laughter again.

I remembered the way her face looked the day she told me it was time to stop haunting the earth plane, time to cross the bridge and move on to where our parents and Buttercup waited—her eyes unnaturally bright, her voice much too tight. She'd tried so hard to play it straight, to be mature, to be tough, to do the right thing—but it was easy to see she was just as broken as I was.

The memory blooming so large in my head, it began to feel real. Began to seem as though it was happening all over again.

And I was so caught up in the moment, so caught up in the grief of saying good-bye, that I nearly missed it when Balthazar cried, "Got it! *Perfetto!* Now hurry—*vite-vite,* Riley Bloom! Follow me!"

12

Like a gymnast rotating toward a mat—like a skydiver hurtling toward a welcoming patch of grass—the key to a successful dream jump is all about nailing the landing.

Or, as Balthazar put it: "After the imprint, the landing is everything. Without the perfect landing, the dreamer will wake, and all is kaput!"

According to Balthazar there were no second chances where dreams were concerned. You had to practice until you got it right. And if you couldn't get it right, well, then you had to cut your losses, find your way out of Dreamland, go someplace quiet, and try your luck with a thoughtwave.

I was beginning to realize just what a privilege I'd been handed. Up until that moment, I had no idea that others had been forced to apprentice with the assistant directors for long, untold periods of time before Balthazar would even consider working with them.

alyson noël

"How long did it take Mort to learn?" I asked, not to be competitive, but because I needed something to go on, some kind of time frame for how long it should take me to learn what I needed to know.

But Balthazar just scowled, dismissed my question with an impatient wave of his hand. "Mort is not my concern. Nor is he yours. We have only a short time before closing time comes. If you want a successful dream jump, you must do the work."

I nodded, just about to ask how he could possibly know it was almost closing time in a place where there was no time to speak of, when he looked at me and said, "Enough with your questions. Answers cannot help you when the work is intuitive. So, tell me, are you ready to make your first jump?"

I nodded, part of me excited and eager, the other part quaking with nerves. Unsure if I was up for the challenge when I'd never been all that great at jumping rope, or doing the high jump, or the long jump, or any other activity having to do with *jumping*—and surprised to find that it wasn't really a jump at all. Balthazar was right, the work was intuitive—the jump was way more mental than physical.

Basically I had to observe a whole slew of dreams. Other people's dreams—complete strangers' dreams—not one of whom was even the least bit familiar to me. Balthazar and

I sat side by side, watching a random assortment of images play out on the screen, and it was my job to find just the right moment to pop in and send a message. And, since it was only the first step in my training session, since I wasn't actually jumping into the scene, I just shouted, "Jump!" whenever the time seemed just right.

It took me a while to get the hang of it. It was way, way harder than it might seem. And as soon as I'd graduated from that, Balthazar had me jumping for real.

We moved to a soundstage—one that was smaller than the one where Buttercup had made his debut—one that was used strictly for training—a place where, basically, I did all the same things I'd just done.

I'd watch a dream in progress, but instead of yelling, "Jump!" I'd just nod, and the next thing I knew I was somehow propelled from my seat and projected right into the scene. Dropped right in the middle of whatever it was that was happening, and then, without alerting the dreamer, without startling them, scaring them, or, worst of all, waking them, I had to find a way to blend in, to not stand out in any way.

It seemed like it should be a cinch. The kind of thing that should be impossible to fail. Easy-peasy in every sense of the word.

But, as it turned out, it was pretty much the opposite of the way it first seemed.

On my first three attempts, all of the dreamers woke up.

On the fourth, the dreamer marched right up to me and demanded to know who I was and just how I got there.

And on the fifth—well, that's when I froze. I had no idea what to do.

"Cut!" Balthazar shouted, the sound of his voice yanking me out, propelling me back in my seat, where I cowered beside him. "What have you done? Why you just stand there like that? Like a . . . like a . . . like a *snowman!*"

I bit down on my lip, pretty sure he meant to say *statue* and not *snowman,* but I was so completely ashamed of myself, I was in no position to correct him.

"I'm so sorry." I shook my head, looked away. "I guess . . . I guess I just froze. It felt like I was caught in a nightmare."

He looked at me, brows slanting together as his eyes bulged beneath them. "*Nightmare? Nightmare!* You think I make nightmare? You think I allow that sort of dark dream?"

He was angry.

No, actually it was far worse than that. He'd gone from testy and red-faced to absolutely furious in just a handful of seconds. And I was so desperate for him to understand, so desperate for him to get what I meant, that I said, "No! I didn't mean it was a nightmare for *the dreamer*—I meant that it was a nightmare *for me!*"

He stopped. Squinted. Yanked his notepad from his

back pocket and flipped through the scribbled-up pages, studying them carefully before leveling his gaze back on me.

"That girl—the dreamer—she was at a school dance, right?"

Balthazar frowned.

"Well, as it turns out, I've never been to a school dance. I mean, I've seen them on TV shows and movies and stuff. Even read about them in books. But I've never experienced one for myself. We didn't have any of those at my old school. I guess they figured we weren't mature enough to handle it." I rolled my eyes, shook my head, but then quickly moved on, got back to the point. "They saved that sort of thing for the teens in junior high. And, as luck would have it, I died right before I could get there. Which is why I wasn't sure how to act, or how to blend in. That's why I froze like I did. Like . . . like a *snowman*."

Balthazar considered, grumbled a few foreign phrases I couldn't comprehend, then he shoved the notebook back in his pocket, adjusted his scarf, and said, "You think Russell Crowe was really a gladiator?"

He stared at me, awaiting my reply, but I had no idea what to say. No idea who he was talking about, much less what he was getting at.

"You think Marlon Brando was a member of the mob?"

He scoffed, eyes narrowing to slits as he shook his round head. "You think Elizabeth Taylor was the true queen of the Nile? You think she was the *real* Cleopatra?"

I just stood there, feeling dumber by the second, as Balthazar grumbled some more foreign phrases, before he looked at me and said, "You think, how do you say . . . ?" He squinted, rubbed his chin. "You think that this . . . this . . . Daniel Radcliffe—you think he rides a broom in real life?"

I cringed, shoulders slumping so badly I practically shrank to half my actual size. Suddenly understanding what he meant by all that, but before I could find a reply, he shouted, "*None* of those people were *none* of those things before they shot the scene! But, once they found themselves there, they felt their way through it. They determined what was necessary—what was called for—what to do! This is called *acting,* Riley! And if you want to dream jump, then you must act too. You must adjust to the scene you find your-self in, you must quickly observe all the action around you, and then you must do whatever it takes to fit in . . . to . . . to *blend* . . . to become *one* with the scene! That is what I require of you!"

I straightened my shoulders, and lifted my head. I got it. I really, truly got it. Finally, it all made sense. It pretty much mimicked what I'd thought earlier—if I could *act* it, I could *be* it. And so I was determined to handle it, I was pretty dang sure that I could. All I needed was another chance, though a little direction wouldn't hurt.

My gaze leveling on his in a dead-on stare when I said, "While I agree that's all true, it's also true that another thing all of those people had in common was *a good director.*" I paused, waited for my words to sink in. "Every one of those actors had a *good director* who helped to *guide* them—to *steer* them—who *helped* them find their way."

Balthazar studied me, considered my words, choosing to let me try once again when he shouted, "Fine, now we move on. Scene six, take one—*action!*"

13

It took me a total of nine jumps to nail it.

Nine whole jumps to finally perfect the landing.

But even though I'd succeeded, even though I was feeling pretty dang proud of myself, even though we'd just moved on to the most amazing back lot—the kind with faux cityscapes and street scenes—the kind they use in all the best movies—according to Balthazar, my success came too late.

Closing time had arrived.

Or, as Balthazar put it: "Cut! That's a wrap!"

Those four simple words were all it took for everything to come to a quick and grinding halt.

I stood there, Buttercup beside me, watching a stream of people all heading in the same direction—toward the exit. And yet, despite the evidence before me, I still refused to believe it was over. Refused to believe my big opportunity had ended so easily.

It wasn't my fault it took me so long—I'd gotten a late start! I mean, seriously? Quitting time? How could there even be such a thing—it just didn't make any sense.

But before I could even lodge a complaint, Balthazar was already waving good-bye, already walking away.

Acting as though the time he'd spent coaching me was over in more ways than one.

Acting as though he'd forgotten all about me, and my dog, not to mention my backstory.

He didn't even say good-bye. He just turned on his heel and moved on to whatever came next.

Treating my dream jump like it was just some dumb TV infomercial.

Some low-budget movie headed straight for DVD.

Some crummy YouTube video that wouldn't get a single comment or view.

Some amateur project he'd been forced to waste his great talent on.

Treating Buttercup and me as though we were disposable.

And when a guy walked toward us with the same style scarf and goatee as Balthazar wore, like it was some kind of Dreamland director's uniform, I grabbed hold of his sleeve and yanked hard as I said, "I was hoping you could help me. I was just about to make my dream jump when everything started shutting down for the day."

He squinted, shook his head, and pointed toward the gate a whole swarm of people continued to pour through.

But I wasn't having it. No way would I give up so easily. I'd worked dang hard to perfect my landing, and I was having my dream jump whether they liked it or not.

"Yeah, well, I get that it's quitting time and all." I tried to smile, but it felt pretty fake so I was quick to move on. "I mean, I'd just perfected the landing—I was just about to jump for real, when Balthazar yelled, 'Cut!' and everything stopped, and, well, because of that I still haven't gotten my jump. And the thing is, I'm ready. I know exactly what to do, so this really shouldn't take all that long. So, with that in mind, I was wondering like, what happens next? Can you squeeze me in real quick? Can I come back tomorrow? And if so, do I get to go first?"

He looked at me, his voice gruff and hurried when he said, "You can add your name to the waiting list—Balthazar will get to you when he can." Then he left.

I called after him. Told him I needed a little more to go on than that. But it was no use. The words never reached him.

So I did the only thing I could, I motioned for Buttercup to follow as we headed for the gate too. And even though

I tried to smile and act happy for Mort's benefit, the truth was, I felt deflated. More than a little bit devastated. Unwilling to believe my big chance was over—*kaput*—just like *that*.

"So, how'd it go?" Mort leaned down to pet Buttercup, who happily sniffed and licked his fingers. "Did you learn how to jump? What'd you think of it? You talk to your sister?"

I slunk through the gate, managed to answer his questions as best as I could. Though my heart wasn't in it. And before we'd gotten too far, well, that's when a whole new thought appeared.

It was just a flash, which is all I could really allow since I had no idea how to shield my thoughts from everyone else. But basically I figured since I'd worked so hard to succeed— since I'd done everything that was asked of me—well, I deserved to get what I came for. I had no intention of leaving, no intention of going anywhere, until I got my dream jump. There was no way I'd linger at the bottom of some waiting list—no way at all. That kind of thing wasn't working for me.

"I . . ." I tried not to gulp, fidget, or engage in any other kind of nervous habit that might make Mort and Buttercup suspect a really big lie was in progress. "I . . . uh, I forgot something. I forgot my . . ." I almost said I forgot my *sweater*, but at the last second I remembered how Ever forgot her sky-blue Pinecone Lake Cheerleading Camp sweatshirt at the campsite the day we all died. How my dad turned the car around to go back and get it, and that's when the deer ran in front of us, the car swerved off the road, and the rest, as they say, is history. So instead I just said, "I forgot my bracelet—my silver charm bracelet. I think it fell off when—"

"So you manifest another one." Mort's voice was a little bit edgy, maybe even testy. Now that his dream jump was over he was ready to catch the train and move on. "You know how to do that, right? You just close your eyes and envision it, and . . ."

Buttercup looked at me, head tilted, eyes wide, as though he was tuning in to my devious mind.

So I shook my head, mumbled something about it being one of a kind, having belonged to my sister, that it couldn't be replaced quite so easily. Then I told Mort not to worry about me. Told Buttercup not to wait for me. Assured them both I'd be fine, would catch the next train, or perhaps even fly. Either way, I'd find my way back. I had a few ideas of where to start looking. It might take a while, but I was sure I would find it. No reason to wait. I'd catch them both later.

Then, before they could stop me, I ran.

Ran as fast as I could.

Slipping through the gate when the guard had his back turned, and making my way across the concrete, the grass, and over to the asphalt.

Heading straight for the soundstage without once looking back.

14

While all the soundstages I'd visited back on the earth plane were equipped with the latest high-tech security systems (I knew this from all the time I spent hanging out on movie sets, spying on actors and stuff before I crossed the bridge and moved Here), in the Here & Now, there was no need for that kind of thing.

Everything worked on the honor system.

For one thing, it's not like you could actually steal anything when everything there was to be had could be easily manifested again.

And for another, in case you hadn't already guessed, the Here & Now really isn't the kind of place where you find a lot of criminal activity.

People Here mostly do the right thing. They want to learn and grow and improve.

They want to glow brighter so they can move up as many levels as possible.

Which is why it was so easy for me to sneak my way back inside.

But which is also why I felt so terribly guilty about having done so successfully.

Still, the guilty feeling didn't last all that long. I had a dream jump to get to. I had no time for shame.

I needed to keep moving. I needed to find a way to be thirteen. It couldn't wait any longer—the need was too great.

I headed toward the soundstage, figuring I'd reenact everything Balthazar had taught me. I'd go silent, go quiet, tune in to Ever's energy pattern, her *imprint,* and take it from there.

Maybe I wouldn't have access to all the stunt people and makeup artists, and costumers, and props, and all that— but there was also nothing wrong with keeping it simple.

Short, sweet, and simple—it would get the job done.

I'd spend a little time with my sister, get some good tips, then find my way out.

Easy-peasy.

I brightened at the idea. It felt good to have a plan. Or at least that's what I thought up until it went black.

And I mean *black.*

Like, no lights, no glow, no nothing kind of black.

Even though I hadn't been in the Here & Now all that long, that was the first time I'd ever experienced something like that.

I couldn't remember it ever once getting dark. Everywhere you went there was light to be found. Always sort of radiating with a soft, goldeny, glistening glow. And though I could never spot the source, it was constant, luminous, making it seem as though the entire place was lit from within.

Unless, of course, you wanted to manifest snow, or rain, or wind, or some other type of foul weather (believe it or not, some people actually missed that kind of thing)—but even then it was relegated to a small, selected area that was easy enough to avoid while it played itself out or the person grew bored of it, whichever came first. And in no time at all, everything returned to that soft, beautiful glow once again.

But the kind of all-encompassing, opaque, inky dark I found myself in, well it was the sort of thing I hadn't seen since our family camping trips back on the earth plane. And even then, we still had the moon. We still had the stars to shine down upon us.

But in Dreamland there was nothing like that. And when I tried to manifest a flashlight, and then a whole armful of flashlights, it barely made a dent in the heavy canopy of black velvet sky.

I should probably admit right now, that that was pretty much the moment when I started to have second thoughts. I'd never been a fan of the dark—especially the pitch-black kind of dark—the kind of dark that can't be easily cured.

I started to leave, was more than willing to cut my losses and *vámanos* myself right out of there. The night felt so threatening, so ominous, that the idea of lingering on a really long waiting list was starting to look pretty good.

But just because I was willing to leave doesn't mean I was able. When I lifted my own hand before me, held it before my eyes and wiggled my fingers, well, I couldn't even see it. It was as though I'd lost all my digits.

With no way of knowing whether or not I was headed in the right direction, I resorted to baby steps. Small, timid, baby steps. All the while cursing myself for sending Buttercup off on his own, for telling Mort I could handle it fine. Picking up the pace when the panic started to mount, and regretting the decision the moment I crashed straight into a wall. Crashed so hard I was sure I'd just made my semi-stubby nose even stubbier.

I stood there, palms pressed to my face, my entire body shaking as I choked back the tears. Stealing a moment to give myself a very stern talking-to, reminding myself that fear was for sissies, panic led to no good, and crying was an indulgence I could not afford.

Repeating it again and again until it started to feel real—until I started to believe.

And that's when I saw it.

The tiniest, briefest flicker of light.

It was quick.

Fleeting.

Here and gone in an instant.

Still, it was enough to convince me to wait patiently, silently—hoping with all of my might that I'd see it again.

The second time was as brief as the first, but it was enough to get me moving—enough to convince me to take one more baby step toward the source. Stopping each time it went dark, then taking another step forward when that quick beam of light pierced through, then stopping the second it went black once again.

It felt like forever before I reached it. Though by that point I was just glad to have made it, even though I had no idea where I might be.

I stood outside the building, ran my hand along the coarse, rough wall, pretty sure it wasn't one of the ones I'd already visited—overcome with the sinking, dreaded feeling that it just might be the building I'd glimpsed earlier.

The one that looked old.

Run-down.

Forgotten, abandoned, and left to rot in a way that should've been condemned.

And when the light flashed again, I saw where it came from. Saw the way it slipped through the cracks of an old, boarded-up space that probably once held a door.

I edged toward it, smooshed my cheeks against the splintery slats, and peered in. Startled to find a kid I guessed to be about my age—a boy with hair so blond it was practically white, and skin so pale it blended into the hair. And when he turned, when he looked in my direction and his gaze settled on mine, I saw that his eyes were so deep and blue they reminded me of California swimming pools.

With the blond hair, blue eyes, and pasty pale skin, he wasn't all that different from me—and yet, his features seemed so exaggerated, so startling and unexpected, I couldn't decide if he looked like an angel . . .

Or more like its opposite.

I froze, unsure what to do. But before I could do much of anything, he'd already jumped from his chair, already moved to the place where I stood.

A couple of distressed pieces of wood the only things standing between us, as he placed his hands on his hips and said, "You're not supposed to be here." His voice was much higher than I would've expected, but deadly serious nonetheless.

I nodded. There was no use denying what we both knew was true.

"No one's supposed to be here after closing."

I shrugged, folded my arms across my chest, and peered past his shoulder. Trying to think of something to say that might get him to lighten up, let me hang around for a bit, at least until the darkness went away.

But the second I met his eyes, I knew those words would never come. There was something very odd about him, something I couldn't quite put my finger on.

"Usually the dark does the trick. It's enough to keep all the stragglers away. That's the whole point, you know. That's why it happens. And yet, here you are."

I bit down on my lip, did my best to hold on to his gaze.

"I guess you don't scare easily, then?"

I squared my shoulders, recognizing a challenge when I heard one. Clearly he had no idea just who he was dealing with, and maybe it was time that I told him—heck, maybe I should even *show* him.

Big bad ghosts were my specialty. I'd already dealt with quite a few. From what I knew, the really bad ones were all lingering down on the earth plane, so how bad could this blond kid be if he was hanging out Here, in some old, abandoned soundstage?

I was tempted to roll my eyes, but I made myself refrain. Figuring at best, he was just some silly wannabe—at worst, he actually thought he could scare me.

Puh-leese.

"Yeah, I get it." He looked me over carefully. "Fear is for sissies, right?"

I looked at him and shook my head. I'd been so distracted by my own thoughts, I wasn't sure if I'd heard him right.

"What?" I squinted, taking him in, or at least what the slats allowed me to see. Not getting much more than a glimpse of a crisp, white shirt that was worn with the kind of pants, belt, and shoes my dad used to wear for important meetings at work. Shaking my head yet again at how some of these ghosts continued to dress despite the fact that they could manifest whatever they wanted.

But he just smiled, removed a few slats, and waved me right in. Motioning for me to crouch low so I wouldn't hit my head, then he replaced those slats again. "I asked if you were here about a dream," he said.

I stood before him, pretty sure that's not at all what he'd said. But thinking he might be able to help, that if I played it just right, then I might still get what I came for, I decided to let that one go.

"You know, come to think of it . . ." He paused, his grin growing wider. "I could use a little help around here. So, how about you help me with my dream jump, and then I'll help you with yours. Deal?"

He extended his hand, waiting for me to shake it.

So I did.

I ignored my better instincts and clasped it in mine.

15

He told me his name was Satchel.

Satchel Alexander Blaise III.

And I stood right before him, listening to him recite it, completely impressed.

The name sounded weighty. Important. Like he might descend from royalty or something.

But Satchel just shrugged. Assured me it was just a name that'd been passed down in the family until it was his turn to wear it, not so different from a hand-me-down shirt.

Assured me that it didn't mean much of anything, so I shouldn't attach too much meaning to it.

There were other things that mattered more.

"*Much* more," he said.

"Yeah, like what?" My gaze pored over him, hoping the answer might help me get to know him a little better, might prove that there was nothing to be afraid of, that he was really no different from me.

Hoping that it might rid me of the creepy, nagging feeling that had stirred up inside me ever since I made my way in and grasped his hand in mine.

But he just shrugged again, saying, "We'll get to that later. First, I need help with this dream."

He led me deeper into the room, and finally I saw where that strange and flickering light had originated. He had some antique projector rigged up in the back that pointed toward a big, stained old screen—its corners all yellowed and curled, with a series of rips and tears that crept along the bottom seam.

"What's this?" I asked, thinking this room was so much smaller than the one I'd done my practice jumps in, and wondering why he was using such old, outdated equipment when there was shiny, new, modern stuff to be had, if not manifested.

"New is not always better." He glanced at me, fiddled with the cuffs of his sleeves. "This works just as well, and besides, it's authentic."

I stopped right there, refusing to take another step closer. "Authentic to *what*, exactly?" My hand on my hip, my lips screwed to the side, needing a bit more to go on.

He huffed, patted his hair with the palm of his hand—smoothing a haircut that wasn't just totally and completely outdated, but that also looked as though it was whipped into obedience with superglue and spit.

"Authentic to Dreamland," he said. "This, all that you see before you, it's all of the original equipment. It's what they used to use before . . ." He paused, then, shaking his head, decided to leave it right there.

Though I wasn't about to let him off so easily. If he needed help, then I needed answers, despite whatever deal we may have struck just a few moments earlier.

I narrowed my eyes, fixed him with my most serious, stoniest stare. Watching as he sighed, threw his arms in the air, and said, "*This* is the stuff they used to use before things changed around here. This is all the original equipment that . . ."

And that's when I knew. Knew it before the words left his lips.

His eyes locked on mine as he confirmed the thought in my head.

"This is the stuff the dreamweavers used back in the day."

Dreamweaving.

According to the gate guard, Mort, and most definitely

Balthazar, dreamweaving was not done in these parts anymore. Heck, I'd gotten a major case of the stink-eye just for
making an accidental mention of it.

I looked at Satchel, my eyes growing wide. But he just
smiled, his face radiant, almost angelic, when he said, "Trust
me, once you weave a dream, you'll never want to dream
jump again."

16

"The secret to dreamweaving is to keep the ingredients as organic as possible. It needs to come off as real and authentic, otherwise the dreamer will wake and the message will fail. With dreamweaving you have to make it seem like something the dreamer would've come up with by themselves—something they'd never even guess was not their own creation. Dreamweaving is all about leaving a big impression. It's all about the impact you make."

I nodded, committing his words to memory, wondering if I should maybe manifest myself a small notebook so I could scribble it down, just like Balthazar had done with my backstory.

"Don't get me wrong," Satchel said, nodding at me. "You can use all the monsters, dragons, witches, warlocks, fairies, werewolves—whatever fantasy creatures you like—as long as it's *real* to the dreamer—as long as it's part of their experience, part of their world. As long as it's something they either secretly, or not so secretly, believe in. If it's real to them, then it's fair game. It's all about *knowing* the dreamer. Knowing what they *care* about . . . what they *desire* . . . what they *fear*. Or, in many cases, what they *overlook*."

I squinted, wondering how he could possibly know all of this. But just as soon as I'd completed the thought, he smiled and said, "I studied under Balthazar."

I gasped, wondering how that could possibly be when I figured him for the same age as me. And then it hit me—maybe he *was* the same age as me.

Maybe he had been the same age as me for a very long time.

Maybe there was no way to grow and mature.

Maybe Bodhi had lied about all that in an attempt to get me to shut up and stop complaining about being eternally twelve.

Maybe we really were stuck.

Maybe I'd live Here for infinity and nothing about me would change!

"I was his number-one intern," Satchel said, invading my thoughts, but I was happy to let him, they were putting me into a serious mental tailspin. "I was the best assistant director Dreamland ever saw . . ."

"And then?" I gulped, eager to hear what came next.

He shrugged, patted his hair, a gesture he'd done twice in the short time I'd known him, and I wondered if it was his own personal nervous *tell*.

"And then . . ." He paused, tugged at the cuffs on his shirt (another tell?), took way too much time inspecting his sleeve, pretending to remove a nonexistent piece of lint. "And then, we had a disagreement." He shrugged. "A sort of . . . *falling out,* if you will. And now Balthazar does what he does—*dream jumps*—and I do what I do—*dreamweaving.* Trust me, Riley, my way is better. You're lucky you found your way here. Balthazar has talent, there's no doubt about that. But what he lacks is *vision.* And whether you're directing a dream, or a movie, or even a play you put on for you parents and your dog in your garage . . ."

He looked right at me, and I wondered how he could possibly know about that, how he could possibly know about Ever's and my Rainy Day Productions—that's what we called our theater company, we even made brochures to go with it. But then he just smiled again, and I began to relax, figuring lots of kids did stuff like that. It was an easy guess on his part.

"Anyway," he continued, reclaiming my attention. "No matter what sort of production you're directing, vision is *everything.*"

I looked at him, remembering how Balthazar had

claimed that *the imprint* was everything, and that *the landing* came a close second. Clearly they worked from two very different perspectives.

"What Balthazar does is nice, don't get me wrong," Satchel continued. "And it definitely serves a purpose, there's no doubt. But, as you're about to see, there's just no comparison. His stuff . . . well, it's a little *schmaltzy*. A little . . . *sappy*. Too many rainbows and smiling puppies for sure. His stuff is dripping with sugar, and spice, and everything nice. Overly sentimental in the most obvious way." He grimaced, making clear his disapproval, his distaste. "It's not near as important as the work I do here. The same work you'll soon be doing here too. What I do changes lives, Riley. After one of my dreamweaves . . . well, let's just say that the dreamer's life is never quite the same. They begin to see their place in the world in a whole new way."

I looked at him, wondering if Balthazar knew he was here, wondering if anyone knew he was here.

"So, what do you say we get started?" he said, not allowing me enough time to reply before he added, "Oh, and just so you know, there is no dream jumping here. There's no need for it. What I do covers everything."

"So, how do you do it?" I asked, more intrigued than anything. Following the curve of his arm, all the way down to the tip of his slim, pale finger as he pointed toward a dark, empty stage with the stained screen right behind it.

"For starters, you need to head over there. Stand right on your mark. You'll see it when you get there. And then I'll start the projector, and you just sort of . . . go with it. Remember how you did with the dream jump? Well, that part's the same. You just keep on acting no matter what. You stay in character until I tell you to stop. Deal?" He looked at me, looked directly into my eyes, and all I could do was nod in reply.

That was the second time he'd used the word "deal." And while I liked it even less than the first time, for some reason, I didn't hesitate to do what he said. It's as though his gaze alone was compelling me forward. Like I no longer controlled my own will. But what was even stranger is that I didn't seem to care. I only wanted to please him, to get a good review.

"Like this?" I asked, my voice too high, my smile too bright. "Is this the right spot?" Knowing it was. The X was clearly marked. And yet, I couldn't help but seek his approval, even if it took a little begging on my part.

He nodded, face squinched in deep concentration as he peered between the viewfinder and me, saying, "Now remember, it's like Balthazar taught you. Just go with the scene you find yourself in. Adapt and blend in, no matter what I put before you, no matter what the situation. Just do whatever it takes to make sure the dreamer stays in the scene too. The last thing we want is for them to wake up before the dream is complete. There's a very important message attached, I don't just make this stuff up for my own entertainment, you know. But, it's imperative they experience the *whole, entire* dream. It's imperative that they don't wake prematurely. Otherwise, the message will be lost."

I nodded, staring at my feet, making sure they didn't stray from the mark. Then my eyes flicked toward the screen and I focused as hard as I could. Body on edge, senses on high alert, waiting for an image to appear, waiting for my cue to begin.

The first thing I heard was the odd click and whir as the film reel circled. Then the screen went pitch-black, but only for a second before it lit up again, bearing an image of an old Indian wearing a headdress perched above a series of circles containing a bunch of seemingly random numbers. I squinted, trying to think of where I'd last seen that, and then I remembered, it was an old TV test pattern. Back on the earth plane, my friend Emily's brother had a T-shirt with the exact same picture on it.

And then, just like *that,* the next thing I knew the screen lit up with the most spectacular thunder and lightning show, and I stood there in awe, happy to watch, and feeling pretty thankful it remained on the screen, that it wasn't actually raining on me.

Though unfortunately, the thought came too soon, and the next thing I knew it was raining for real. Like taking a ride through the car wash in a convertible with the top left down, a torrential downpour completely drenched me.

When the lights up above started to sizzle and crack, their bulbs popping and flaring as though they might electrocute me, I took to the ground and ducked my head low. Doing what I could to shield myself with my hands by grasping them tightly over my head, silently reciting the facts as I knew them: The Here & Now didn't run on electricity—it was just some kind of special effect—part of the dream Satchel was weaving—there was no way any of it could harm me.

I peered toward him, knowing better than to look at the camera, much less at the director, while in the middle of shooting a scene, unless, of course, you were directed to. But still I glanced his way, squinting through steady ribbons of water raining down all around me, hoping for a little direction, a little approval—looking for some indication of where this scene might be heading, and just how long I'd be required to put up with this—but not getting much of anything.

Satchel was absorbed. Having moved away from the projector, he'd perched himself behind a big, old-timey computer where he punched furiously on its keyboard. No longer taking notice of me—his lack of attention left me feeling really sad and empty.

I wanted him to notice, to approve of my acting, to applaud my hard work. I wanted him to cast me in all of his future productions, give me the starring role. I really, really, really wanted him to be proud of me.

Though, I had no idea why.

My mind began to ponder, wondering why some weird kid's approval was worth getting drenched over. And just as I began to grab hold of myself, questioning why I was staying, if I might not be better off leaving, I heard panting.

Heavy, frantic, grunting and panting.

Then a second later I realized it came from the girl running toward me.

The girl running toward me with the filthy, ripped-up clothes, stringy, wet hair, and terrified face.

I started to shout. Decided I'd play the part of a Good Samaritan—or a hero even. I started to tell her not to worry, that I was there to help. But the second I opened my mouth, the words all backed up in my throat.

Sticking.

Clogging.

Like a drain all jammed up with gunk.

My toes were sinking. The shoes I once wore were no more. Everything had changed.

Every. Single. Thing.

I was no longer standing on a stage. The black painted wood that had, just a moment before, been supporting me, had turned into something very different—something I once saw in a really old movie.

Sandy, soggy, and swampy—I immediately recognized it as quicksand. And I knew if I didn't move fast, in no time at all it would swallow me whole.

With the scream still lodged in my throat, I did my best to run. But every step forward was a useless endeavor. The sand was too quick, too deep. It was dragging me down—sucking me in, forcing its way up to my nose and into my mouth.

But if I thought I had it bad, well, that was nothing compared to the girl. Not only was she sinking up to her neck, but a whole team of alligators had appeared out of no-where. Their powerful, crunching jaws yawning open and snapping shut as though it was a warm-up, as though they were preparing to devour her.

I freed my hand of the muck and lurched toward her. Urging her to lean toward me, to take hold if she could. I tried to smile, tried to nod in encouragement, to give her a reason to fight, to not give up until we'd exhausted every last resource. Watching as she thrust her body toward mine, the alligators charging, snapping, chomping on air, hoping to soon replace it with pieces of her.

And then, just when she was near, just when our fingers met and she'd grabbed ahold of me, a searing hot flame tore through her flesh, giving me no choice but to let go.

I couldn't help it—it just sort of happened—it was a reflex—it wasn't my fault! And when I tried to reach her again, it was too late.

She was gone.

The gators had claimed her.

My throat cleared. The scream, finally uncorked, rang out all around until I grew hoarse and it played itself out. And I was just about to renew it, hoping someone would hear me, help me, when I opened my eyes and saw everything had changed once again.

The rain had stopped.

The quicksand was gone.

And I found myself standing on a patch of freshly mown grass, getting ridiculed loudly by a small group of teens for having just screamed my head off.

I shrank back, shrank back into myself, into the shadows so they could no longer see me, though I could see

them. Taking a quick look around, I did what I could to as-
sess the new situation I found myself in. Remembering
what Satchel had said, that no matter what happened, I
had to stick with it, it was the only way the message could
be sent.

I was in a park. A park after dark, which meant the little
kids had already vacated, were already at home, safely tucked
into their beds, while a gang of unruly teenagers took over,
littering the sandbox with cigarette butts, and making rude
drawings all over the slide.

The kind of teens I never wanted to be—always did
my best to avoid—taking great pains to keep a wide distance between us whenever I'd see them lurking in my old
neighborhood on my way home from school.

The kind of teens that made trouble, listened to no one,
"flaunted authority," as my mom would've said.

The kind of teens that pretty much wrecked it for all of
the others.

And even though I knew it was my job to find a way to
fit in, to blend, all I really wanted was to sit this one out.

I cowered in the dark, huddled up next to the bathrooms,
hoping that unfortunate scream of mine was enough to scare
them off.

For a while anyway, it worked.

Until the big four-wheel-drive with no driver flipped on its brights and tried to mow us all down.

I ran.

We all did.

Though we didn't get very far. Unlike the last dream, in this one, my feet didn't so much sink as stick. The freshly mowed grass turning into a goopy, green, superglued mess that held fast to the bottoms of our shoes, refusing to release us, refusing to free us. Even the ones who'd stepped out of their shoes were no better off—they'd merely replaced the soles of their shoes with the soles of their feet.

All I could do, all any of us could do, was stare helplessly into the truck's headlights as it ran us all down.

At the moment of impact, there was an amazing flash of bright light, and the next thing I knew, I was in Paris, a city I'd always wanted to visit. But instead of sightseeing and riding the elevator to the top of the Eiffel Tower, I was drowning in the River Seine along with a group of loitering teenagers.

Then, the next thing I knew, I was in Brazil, only instead of spending a nice day baking in the sun, I was being roasted for real—a young girl, two boys, and me going up in flames on a Rio de Janeiro beach.

I suffered through nightmares in all of the most exotic places. Places I'd always wanted to visit. Then just as I began longing for home, my wish was granted. I found myself in school—my old school—standing in front of my old class. And when I gazed down at myself, wondering what they were all pointing and laughing about, well, that's when I realized I'd forgotten to dress.

I froze, figuring I'd die right there on the spot of complete mortification—but then a second later I found myself wearing a cute purple dress I definitely approved of, while sitting at a desk in that very same class. Concentrating hard on the paper before me—part of a very important, grade-making test—unable to read, much less answer, even one single question, all of the words swimming before me in a big, foggy blur.

I raised my hand, about to ask if I could get a new test, explain that there was something wrong with the one that I had—when I saw that my teacher wore the face of a clown, and the body of a black widow spider. Her eight legs and arms trapping me in her web, gazing upon me as though I was dinner.

I screamed.

I railed.

I fought as hard as I could—but it didn't do the slightest bit of good.

I was devoured by insects.

I was buried alive.

I was chased by knife-wielding zombies who snacked on my brains.

Every scene was different—but, in the end, it was all the same thing. Every time a nightmare ended, a new one jumped into its place. It was one assault after another—one terrifying experience quickly followed by the next.

Some were normal fears—some were outrageous—but all of them penetrated to the deepest part of me.

I'd died once in real life—but as long as I was up on that stage, I'd die many more times, in much worse ways.

And the worst part was, there was nothing I could do to stop it. Nothing I could do to make it go away.

All I could do was go with it.

Blend in.

Act my little heart out and let the dreamer decide when to say when.

So completely terrified by the circumstances, it took me a while to realize there was no actual dreamer.

The last five scenes had starred only me.

But no matter how hard I screamed—no matter how hard I fought to break character, to "wake up"—no matter how much I risked Satchel's good opinion of me—it didn't do the least bit of good.

The nightmares continued to loop.

The projector continued to whir.

And each new scene I was thrust into was far worse than the one that went before.

I was trapped.

Stuck in an eternal dance.

Living the never-ending story of all the worst nightmares known to man.

17

Whatever hold Satchel had held over me was long gone.

He'd gotten exactly what he wanted—controlling me was no longer necessary.

I was stranded.

Alone.

Trapped in the web of his horrifying dreamweave. The irony being that with my free will fully restored, I had no way to exercise it. No way to release myself.

I was a prisoner. Completely dependent on whatever shred of mercy Satchel might've had. Though I knew, way down in the deepest part of me, that any hope of mercy was futile.

The place where Satchel's mercy might've lived was as bleak as the place I'd found myself in.

Though there was no denying I alone was to blame.

I'd ignored my better instincts—just pushed them aside so I could go after my own selfish pursuits. Unwilling to play by the rules, unwilling to wait for my turn, I'd shunned everything I'd been told and ran full speed ahead toward my own goals, my own plans, determined to do it my own way. And I'm sad to admit it wasn't the first time I'd done such a thing.

Far from it.

While my only real goal had been to find a quick and easy way to progress myself into being thirteen—in the end, the only thing I'd accomplished was turning myself into the opposite—a scared little kid.

From the moment I'd taken Satchel's hand—from the moment my palm pressed against his, I'd not only sealed our deal—but also my fate.

Without even knowing it, I'd allowed Satchel to take charge of my destiny.

The bad dreams continued, and it wasn't long before I found myself caught in the all-too-familiar "falling nightmare"—tumbling through a deep, dark abyss—body flailing, spiraling through an infinite pool of bottomless blackness. And I couldn't decide which was worse—my having tried so hard to please him, to garner his approval, as I'd done from the start—or my having to face the sudden realization that I was stuck—undeniably aware of the big bad mess I'd put myself in.

I shut my eyes, folded my arms across my chest, and vowed to stop fighting—to just allow it to happen no matter what came my way. In my job as a Soul Catcher I'd dealt with menacing ghost boys before, and I knew the kind of scaredy-cat behavior I'd been displaying only made things worse—only fueled their fun.

For whatever reason, Satchel, just like the others before him, got some kind of sick thrill by scaring people—anyone and everyone from those poor, vulnerable sleepers to me.

Fear.

That's what this whole thing was about. Satchel was driven by fear, and he was determined to make me fearful too.

The best way to end it, the best way to suck the wind right out of his sails, was to refuse to take part. I just hoped it wouldn't take too long for him to bore with his game.

I stuck to my guns—no matter what sort of monster he chose to menace me with—I just kept my eyes closed, kept my arms folded, and refused to take part. And, after a while, after a *long* while, much longer than I'd hoped for, he stopped.

He stopped the projector, stopped everything, until I found myself alone on the stage, strangely enough still right on my mark, as he stood before me, a dark, ominous glare taking over his face.

And when he flipped on the overhead lights, well, that's when I saw it.

That's when I was finally able to pinpoint just exactly what it was I found so weird about him.

He had no glow.

No glow at all.

In fact, not only was his glow missing—it was much worse than that.

The space all around him, the place where the glow should've been, was a complete absence of light—resulting in a murky, dark haze that hovered around him.

I coiled back in fear. Then seeing the way that murky, dark haze began to expand and flare as a result, I grabbed ahold of myself. My fear was exactly what drove him. And if I wanted to get through this, I'd have to refuse to react to whatever came next—just like I'd done with the last several nightmares I'd been cast in.

I clutched my hands on my hips, looked at him, and said, "So, Satchel, what's your deal? What's with all the night-mares? This how you get your kicks—scaring the *beejee-mums* out of innocent, sleeping kids?"

He glared at me, blue eyes raging. "You think you know everything!" he shouted. "You think you're *sooo* smart, don't you?"

I started to respond, started to deny it was true, but the fact is, it wasn't the first time I'd been accused of that. Bodhi had said pretty much the exact same thing—on more than one occasion. So I just stood silently before him, deciding to let Satchel finish his rant with no interruption from me.

"You don't get it. You don't get it *at all*! Nobody does. But that's neither my problem nor my fault." He dug his hands deep into his pockets, pacing in circles until he stopped and faced me again. "I was doing good work. I was really changing lives. Making a huge difference in the way people handled themselves, and the decisions they made. But then . . ." He paused, grimaced, rubbed a palm over his spit-shined hair. "But then the . . . the powers that be, the *Council*"—he pronounced the word with a disrespectful sneer—"they didn't like it. They didn't approve. And the next thing you know, dreamweaving is frowned upon and dream jumping is in." He scoffed, shook his head, made a face like he was about to hock a big ol' loogie, but in the end, settled for just looking at me instead. "But they can't stop me. Nobody can. They can impose closing hours, make this place as dark and uninviting as they want, but they can't stop me from doing what I do best. You do realize that no one will come for you, right, Riley? You do realize there is no white knight ready to rescue you from big bad me. Nothing is forbidden Here. *No. Thing.* We progress—if that's what you want to call it," he rolled his eyes, "at our own pace. And some of us choose not to progress at all. They can't force you to do anything Here. Free will is king, and I'm exercising mine."

Other than a nervous blink, I didn't allow myself to react. What he'd said was all true. Or at least the part about nobody forcing anyone to do anything—I knew that from Soul Catching. I wasn't allowed to evict a ghost from the place they chose to haunt, nor was I allowed to physically push them across the bridge so I could cross them off my list (though there were definitely times I was tempted). All I could ever do was get to know them, build some kind of trust with them, then find a way to *coax and convince* them to move on to the place where they truly belonged.

And that's exactly what I had to do with Satchel.

I had to treat him like the lost soul that he was.

Maybe he'd found his way across the bridge, but from the looks of things, it was hardly enough. From what he'd said, he'd been doing this for far too long, and it was up to me to stop him.

The thought spun in my head.

It was up to me to stop him!

Surely Satchel was on the Council's to-do list, and if I could just find a way to get him to quit terrorizing people—if I could just find a way to get him to find a better, more productive way to exist, well, then surely that would earn me some major kudos and congrats, if not more . . .

What better way to get what I wanted?

What better way to get my glow to glow even brighter?

I'd reduce, if not stop, the nightmares that found their way out into the world, which, in turn, would cause me to leap a heckuva lot closer to my one and only goal.

Being thirteen was finally in reach.

All I had to do was get inside his head. Figure out the reason why he did what he did.

Everyone is driven by something. No one does stuff just for the heck of it. There's always a reason, some kind of motivation. Peer pressure, revenge, the pursuit of world domination or fame, whatever—the motivation's the fuel that sparks the flame—the driving force behind just about everything. All I had to do was learn Satchel's, then quickly dismantle it, show him all the reasons why it just didn't work.

"So, tell me, how exactly are you changing lives by scaring people?" I asked, hoping to get a glimpse inside his sick and twisted head.

Satchel looked at me, his expression open, simple, though if you looked close enough, you could see his blue eyes were simmering just underneath.

"People don't fear enough," he said.

I squinted, thinking of all the things I was afraid of: clowns, spiders, quicksand, accidentally going to school naked—he'd pretty much nailed them all. The only thing he'd left out was dentists and, oh yeah, snakes, though I wasn't about to share that with him.

"People act with abandon. They take unnecessary risks. They think they'll live forever and so they take their lives for granted. They ignore just how extremely dangerous the world really is."

Although he tried to appear outwardly calm, it was clear he was growing agitated. I could tell by the way his fingers twitched and fiddled with the tip of his belt, as his mouth pulled and jumped at the sides.

So I kept my voice steady, low, reluctant to add to his distress, when I said, "Really?" I scratched at my chin as though I was truly considering his words. "Because I'm just not sure I see it that way."

His face went stony, his voice grew snotty, and he said, "Oh really? Then let me ask you this—how did *you* die? How'd you end up Here?" He arched his brow in challenge.

I shrugged, refused to get riled up. "Car accident," I said. "They're pretty common, you know."

He shook his head, shot me a look like I was too dumb to be believed. "Just because they're common doesn't mean they have to be." He shuffled his feet, rocked back and forth before me.. "People don't pay attention. They allow themselves to get distracted by the stupidest things! They mess with the radio, look for stuff they dropped under the seat. Women put on their makeup, and men shave. And now, ever since they invented cell phones," he rolled his eyes and sighed, "people actually send e-mails and text! They do all of these things when they should have their eyes on the road and *only* the road. You should *never, ever* take your eyes from the road! *No matter what!*"

His voice grew louder, firmer, as he reached the end of his rant. Sounding almost as though those last words didn't actually belong to him—as though he was borrowing from some other source.

A source that just might hold the key, but before I could get to that, he asked, "So tell me, who was driving the day you died?"

"My dad," I told him, my voice nearly a whisper.

"*And . . . what happened?*"

I sucked in a mouthful of air, allowed it to bubble my cheeks, before releasing it in a long, slow whistle. "Deer ran in front of the car. Next thing I knew, we were all dead. Well, except for my sister. She died for a bit, but then she found her way back to the living. It's a long story." I shrugged, doing my best to keep to the facts, keep it free of any emotion I may have felt at the time.

He waved his hand impatiently. He had no interest in those kinds of details.

"What I meant is, at the very last second, right before the impact, *what happened*?" His eyes blazed on mine.

I paused for a moment to think, or at least I pretended

to think. The fact is, I'd replayed the scene so many times in my head it was always at the ready, not the least bit difficult to locate. And though I was reluctant to share it with him, knowing it'd be like handing over the perfect scenario for him to use against me—I did it anyway. Figuring a little honesty on my part could only build trust, or at least I hoped that it would.

"I'd just been fighting with my sister." I looked right at him. "My dad peered in the rearview mirror, they exchanged a look, and then, a few seconds later the deer appeared and . . . that's it. It happened pretty fast."

Satchel nodded as though I'd just proved his point. "See? You distracted him." His pale eyebrows quirked as he flashed me a gruesome, triumphant grin.

"So you're implying it was *my* fault?" I tried to keep my voice calm, tried to smother the slow, simmering rage building inside me. "I mean, seriously, you're actually *blaming* me for what happened to my family?"

Satchel studied his hands, inspected his nails. He'd said all that he needed to. The damage was done.

"Maybe some things are just *meant to be*. Maybe some things just happen, *no matter what*. Did you ever think of *that*?" I glared at him, remembering how my sister, Ever, was consumed with blaming herself for our deaths, and how I finally convinced her of all the things I'd just said, how those words served to free her, even if she didn't completely believe them.

But Satchel remained unimpressed. Refused to see things my way.

"Maybe. Maybe not," he said. "All I know for sure is that the dreams *I* weave wake people up. My dreamweaves help people realize just how small, vulnerable, and fragile they really are. They make people cautious. They make them think twice. And despite what you think, none of those kids are *innocent*. That girl that got eaten by the alligators?" He looked at me. "She does things near that swamp with her boyfriend that she knows she shouldn't be doing. Bad things. Dangerous things. Things her parents have warned her about. But now, after my dreamweave, she'll think twice about her actions. She won't be doing that kind of thing again." He flashed a self-satisfied smirk and continued, "And those kids in the park? They hang out there almost every night, drinking, smoking, and getting in fights. I sent that dream to the whole group of them, and I one-hundred-percent guarantee you that once they get talking about it—once they exchange notes and realize they all saw the same thing—they'll be so scared, and rightfully so, that they'll stop all the nonsense, stop abusing their bodies, stop wrecking it for everyone else, and live a better life. And if not, well then I'll just keep chasing them down. I'll just keep dreamweaving exclusively for them, until

they finally get it, or they end up Here prematurely, whichever comes first. And the same goes for everyone else."

He paused, allowing me a chance to react, but I just
held my tongue.

"I'm doing good work here, Riley—work that I should
be rewarded for. But *some* people are just too shortsighted
to see the value in that. You're lucky you met me, you know.
You may already be dead, so there's no sparing you that,
but you're reckless. You think you're way smarter than you
are. You think you know more than anyone else. And, well,
think of it like this, maybe I'm here to save you from yourself." He laughed, though the sound was so icky, so greasy, I
couldn't help but cringe. "I mean, think about it. Think
about everything I just said. Isn't that how you got here?
Isn't that what convinced you to sneak back into Dreamland despite that it was closing time—despite what you'd
been told?"

He paused.

I shrugged.

Clearly we'd reached an impasse.

Until he said, "So tell me, Riley, tell me the truth. I'm
curious, after everything you've experienced here, do you
still think *fear is for sissies*?"

His eyes focused on mine, focused in the way they
had before: piercing, mesmerizing, willing me to seek his

approval, to do whatever it took to please him, to do his bidding.

And though that no longer worked, when I tried to flee, well, that's when I realized the nightmare hadn't really ended.

My feet were nailed to the stage, and my lips were stapled shut.

18

"How does it feel to know no one will come for you?"

Satchel smiled. Having joined me onstage, he proceeded to circle me slowly, to better observe me.

"How does it feel to know you're trapped here? Does it make you feel, oh, I don't know, *fearful,* perhaps?"

With my mouth still stapled shut, it's not like I could answer. But Satchel wasn't in it for the answer. He was in it for the taunt.

"You know, I've been doing this for a very long time, and I must say that you are one of my most challenging dreamweaves to date." He stood before me, eyes widening as though I'd finally managed to impress me. Too bad I no longer cared about that.

"Just so you know, I didn't always deal in nightmares. I used to let people send whatever kind of message they wanted, whether I approved of it or not. I did my job, did what the client and Balthazar wanted. But then one day, I'd had enough of all the softly whispered, sappy encouragements of 'Live your life to the fullest!'

"And worse: 'Seize each day as though it's your last!'"

He rolled his eyes and shook his head. "What complete and utter nonsense—not to mention damaging too! But Balthazar loved it, and, of course, the Council gave it their golden seal of approval. Only *I* could see what was really happening. Only *I* could see the consequence of such a thing. Those supposedly heartwarming dreamweaves were doing more harm than good. They were endangering people, making them believe in a false sense of security. Resulting in a population of delusional people, running around, taking unnecessary risks. *And I think we all know that nothing good comes of that!*"

There was that voice again. The one I'd heard earlier—the one that sounded like he was reciting someone else's words.

And though I was making progress with loosening the staples on my mouth, I didn't let on. I figured I'd stay where I was and let him lead me straight into the good stuff.

"You can send comfort but not prophecy—that's the Dreamland motto in case you didn't know. It's the only real rule we were told to work under. And while it seems to make sense on the surface, while people need to make their own decisions so they can learn and grow, and all that—they also need to make those decisions *with a very clear picture of just how dangerous the world is!* And since no one else was willing to do that—it was up to me to show them."

He stormed the stage, finger jabbing the air every time he said something of particular significance. And the longer he lectured, the more his voice changed, until it was no longer his own. It became someone else's.

He continued to speak, and point, and make all manner of fear-driven statements. His eyes growing so bleary, his expression so foggy, I was pretty sure he was no longer in the present with me, but hung up somewhere in his past.

Not wanting to disturb him or lead him out of his trance, I let the words seep slowly, softly, trailing their way from my head to his, as I thought: *So tell me, tell me just exactly what happened to you that made you this way.*

I stood rigid, letting the thought find its way to his brain.

And because he was who he was—or at least who he claimed to be: the best assistant director Dreamland had ever seen—he decided not to tell me.

He *showed* me instead.

19

The projector whirred as he punched fiercely onto his keyboard. And the next thing I knew, we were dropped into a carnival scene—a sort of old-timey fair.

The kind with clowns, cotton candy, and silly games with cheap prizes that cost only a penny to play.

I gazed down at my clothes, surprised to see myself wearing a flannel skirt with a poodle stitched on it, its hem drooping nearly to the black-and-white saddle shoes on my feet, while on top I wore a snug sweater set with a matching scarf to go with it. Making me look like a character on some 1950s sitcom.

Satchel wore his same white shirt, black pants, shiny belt, and black shoes, and with his spit-slicked hair, and pasty white skin, well, even back then he didn't fit in. Compared to the other boys with their rolled jeans, tight white tees, and sun-warmed skin, he looked more than a little weird. He stood out, in a strange-pale-funeral-director kind of way.

I stood to the side, balancing a cloud of cotton candy in one hand, as I watched him stride alongside his parents. And I have to say that the second I saw them, well it all became clear.

And when his dad began to speak, I knew exactly where *that voice* had come from.

I kept to their pace, walking just behind them, careful to blend in, go completely unnoticed, striving to overhear brief snippets of their conversation.

His mother kept quiet, a vague and distant expression stamped on her unhappy face—while his father, his voice hardened, authoritative, explained all of the very good reasons why Satchel was not allowed to go on any of the rides.

I shoved a wad of cotton candy into my mouth, frowning while I let the little crystallized bits melt on my tongue. Wondering why he'd even bother to take his kid to the carnival if he wasn't allowed to have any fun.

Though it wasn't long before I realized that Satchel had no one else to go with.

Satchel had no friends.

His life consisted only of his parents, schoolwork, and the family's thrice weekly visits to church. And if he was good—very, very good—then maybe they'd allow him to go to a child-friendly movie—an outing that he treasured above everything else. Those moments in a darkened theater, watching a story come to life on a screen, were the only small pleasures he was allowed. Which is more than he could say for his parents, whose lives seemed to hold no pleasure at all.

His mother spent long hours at the ironing board, starching the collars and sleeves of the stiff, white shirts Satchel wore to school and his father wore to work. Satchel's father rose early each day, showered, dressed, and had a quick bite to eat before heading to work. And while Satchel wasn't exactly sure what he did, he knew it had something to do with numbers.

"Numbers are safe—numbers are low risk," his father always said. "If you know how to work 'em, then they always add up in the end."

The carnival was only in town for a week, and all of the kids at school had been talking about it—though of course no one actually mentioned it to him, Satchel had merely overheard them.

He was too weird—too creepy—and he came from a really weird, creepy family—or at least those were the most quoted excuses kids used to avoid him.

But from the moment Satchel glimpsed the tip of the Ferris wheel on a rare trip into town, he wanted nothing more than to see it up close—wanted to see if it was anything like the one in the movie he once saw.

Knowing he wasn't allowed to go on his own (he wasn't allowed to go anywhere on his own except school, church, and the occasional movie, and even then, only during the day—anywhere else was deemed far too dangerous for a boy of thirteen), he'd made a deal with his parents. Promising that if they would just accompany him—then he would agree to not go on any rides, not eat anything made of sugar, and not waste any of his father's hard-earned pennies on games his father claimed were probably rigged anyway.

A promise he had every intention of keeping until he saw her.

Mary Angel O'Conner.

The girl who sat a few rows before him in school—the girl with the glorious mane of long red hair that spilled over the back of her chair like a trail of smoldering embers. Those silken strands gleaming in the slant of noonday sun that crept through the window—appearing so glossy, so inviting, Satchel imagined it would feel like warmed silk in his hand.

Unlike all the other kids, Mary Angel had, on more than one occasion, said a kind word to him. They were moments he'd never forget. Moments he replayed in his head again and again, like a favorite movie.

And there she was, surrounded by a large group of friends, though one glance at Satchel made it clear he saw only her.

I shot a nervous look first at his mom, then at his dad. Hoping they hadn't noticed what had claimed their son's attention, knowing they'd view it as a threat, try to make him fear it. I was already feeling really, really sorry for him.

But they didn't see, they were too busy discussing all the dangers around them, completely unaware of the spark of an idea that just flared in Satchel's mind—one that would've resulted in a hasty stroll toward the exit if they'd had even the slightest inkling of it.

I have to get away from my parents, he thought. *I have to do whatever it takes to rid myself of them. I have to get far, far away—if only for a few seconds.*

He yanked at the cuffs on his shirt, then patted his hair with his hand, two of his usual nervous tells. Deception did not come easily to him.

Carefully steering his parents in another direction, one that was opposite Mary Angel and her friends, he looked first to his mom, and then to his dad, as he said, "I think I just saw someone from school. May I go say hello, please?"

I stood off to the side, polishing off the last sticky strands of cotton candy, while his parents exchanged a worried look. His mother verging on *no,* the most overused word in her vocabulary, some might argue the only word. You could see it engraved on her face, the lines permanently stamped in the place where a smile could've, should've been.

While his father peered closely at Satchel and said, "Who? Who is this person you know from school?"

Knowing the truth would only land him in trouble at best, and back home at worst, he gulped, crossed his fingers behind his back in an attempt to lessen the sting of the lie, and said, "It's just . . . it's just one of the teachers. I want to ask her a quick question about Monday's assignment, that's all."

I veered closer as his parents consulted, listened as they discussed the possible merits along with the very real dangers of allowing him to drift off on his own. And just as his mother was about to say no once again, his father overruled her when he nodded and said, "We'll wait here. Right here. We expect your return in three minutes." Consulting his pocket watch to mark the time. "If you're not back by then, we are coming to get you."

If it'd been me, I would've run like the wind to get the heck out of there, afraid of wasting a single second of such a ridiculously short time frame. But Satchel and I are nothing alike. Which means he didn't run. Didn't even consider it. Running could lead to falling, and falling was bad—a fact that was repeated to him ever since he'd taken his very first step.

With hammering heart, and sweaty palms, he made his way toward her. Having no idea what he'd say once he got there, and knowing all too well there was a good chance that her friends would all laugh, he still had to go through with it. He couldn't let the chance slip away. He was at the carnival—just like any other kid—just like any normal kid—and he wanted Mary Angel to see it.

He wanted her to see him the way he saw her.

By the time he caught up, she and her friends had made their way to the front of the line for the Ferris wheel, waiting for their turn to board.

I stood beside him, the two of us gazing up at the car that loomed highest. And while I'd always loved the Ferris wheel, carnivals too for that matter, Satchel made me see it in a whole different light.

Carnivals were dangerous and dirty places—operated by shady carnies with even shadier pasts—and while all of the rides held their own unique dangers, the Ferris wheel was the granddaddy—the most dangerous of them all. His father had assured him of that on the drive over, while his mother had sat right beside him, head nodding in silent agreement.

I shot him a worried look. He was just a few inches shy of Mary Angel, and I braced for what he might do, what he might say. He was in unfamiliar territory to say the least.

Mary Angel turned, smiling in a way that made her face shine with happiness, and though the smile was in no way directed at him, she'd been merely laughing at something a friend said, Satchel was too sheltered, too hopeful, too socially awkward to see the smile for what it really was.

He used it as an excuse to approach her. Stopping just shy when a boy, Jimmy MacIntyre, otherwise known as Jimmy Mac, or sometimes just Mac, placed a possessive hand on her back, threading his fingers through her blaze of red hair while gently pushing her toward the vacant, waiting car.

"Hey, Satchel, you gonna ride too?" Mary Angel called, finally seeing him as she slid onto the seat.

And though he'd sought her attention, though it was the number-one reason, the only reason, for lying to his parents and risking their wrath if the lie should be discovered— now that she was looking at him, he was struck dumb, left completely speechless, breaking out in a sweat that soon worked its way from his forehead all the way down to his feet.

Jimmy Mac answering for him when he said, "You kidding? Satchel? Ride *this* thing? Please. That kid's such a wimp he has a permanent note to get out of PE. He's not allowed to run! Can you believe it? Running is too dangerous!" He shook his head, rolled his auburn eyes. "Craziest thing I've ever heard and I swear to gawd it's true!"

Mary Angel glanced shyly at Satchel, shot him a regretful look, as Jimmy Mac claimed the space right beside her, his shoulder pressing into her angora-covered shoulder in a way that made Satchel's head swim.

Satchel gulped, gaped, all too aware of the seconds marching forward, erasing all that remained of the three minutes he was given. All too aware of the mountain of trouble that awaited him if he was caught standing anywhere near the mouth of the Ferris wheel.

"You riding or not?" the carnie asked, his face a mess of crags and crevices—evidence of a life lived recklessly, his father would say. And though he knew better than to ask, Satchel wondered how his father might go about explaining his mother, who didn't have much of a life to speak of and yet she bore the same, saddened, used-up look.

"C'mon, get this thing *up!*" Jimmy Mac yelled. "Satchel Blaise the *turd,* oops, I mean the *third,* ain't goin' nowhere. Blaise is the biggest chicken the world's ever seen!"

"Make up yer mind, kid. I don't got all day!" The carnie narrowed his eyes so much they were swallowed by a mass of sallow, puffy, excess skin—the result of too much sun, too many late nights—obviously no one had warned him.

Satchel was just about to turn, just about to head back, knowing his parents were probably already looking for him, probably already steaming mad, when Mary Angel called, "Don't listen to him, Satchel. C'mon, take a ride—the Ferris wheel's fun!"

She wanted him to ride!

Mary Angel—the girl with the fiery red hair and bright shining smile—didn't see him like all the other kids did.

I watched as Satchel threw all caution aside and moved toward the car. My fingers twisting, clutching at each other in a fit of nerves, willing him forward, egging him on, but wanting him to hurry, to board already, before his parents showed up.

He slid into the car below Mary Angel's, getting a quick glimpse of her waving hand, her smiling face, her legs kicking above him. His heart hammering so hard against his rib cage he was sure it would leap right out of his chest and land on his lap. His fingers so slick with sweat, they slipped when he tried to grab hold of the rail and lock himself in, but luckily the craggy old carnie swung by to take care of that for him.

And the next thing he knew he was lifted—carried up—up—up—high into the sky.

Higher than he'd ever been.

Higher than he ever thought possible.

Higher than his parents would ever allow.

But instead of feeling scared, instead of feeling shadowed by imminent danger, he felt exhilarated.

Free.

And for the first time in his life, he gazed down upon the earth, not seeing it as dangerous at all, but instead, as host to the most wonderful possibilities.

His parents were down there somewhere, most likely searching for him. But for the moment, it didn't matter. He didn't care. He refused to think about them. Preferred to concentrate on soaring, the thrill of riding tandem with the clouds. His gaze held fast to the bottom of the red car above him, knowing that Mary Angel soared right along with him.

He dreaded each trip toward the ground, that's where reality lived—and looked forward to each arc into the sky where everything was peaceful and good.

Or at least until Jimmy Mac started rocking his car—rocking it in a way that made Mary Angel let out a shriek, though it wasn't long before that shriek turned into a giggle, and then the giggle into a laugh that went on and on.

Longing to hear that beautiful, soft, lilting laugh directed at him, or rather at something he did, Satchel decided to rock his car as well. Grabbing hold of the sides, he shook it as hard as he could. But instead of laughing, Mary Angel glanced over the side, shooting him a worried, cautious look, while Jimmy Mac cupped his hands around his mouth and yelled, "Hey, Blaise—didn't know you had it in you!" Followed by a few more phrases I missed, but that sent Jimmy Mac into hysterics over his own wit.

But Jimmy Mac hadn't seen anything yet. Satchel had just taken his first bite of freedom and was infatuated with the rush that it gave him. Loved it so much, he craved a steady supply of it.

Thirteen years of being sheltered, and woefully overprotected—thirteen years of cowering from the world—had resulted in thirteen years of pent-up exuberance that longed to get out.

He shook the car again.

Harder.

And then harder still.

Causing Jimmy Mac to hoot and holler, egging him on, as Mary Angel gazed down at him with an increasingly worried frown.

It was an expression that enraged him. Satchel had been raised on worried frowns—had already suffered a lifetime's worth.

He wanted Mary Angel to smile.

He wanted her to laugh in the same way she had for Jimmy Mac.

He shook the car again, much harder than before, causing Mary Angel to scream—yelling something about the security rail.

But Satchel wouldn't listen. Even when she pointed,

begged for him to stop, the sight of her anxious face only spurred him on.

Why was it okay for Jimmy Mac to shake the car, but not him?

Did she agree with all the other kids that he was nothing more than a creepy weirdo wimp?

Did she think he didn't know how to have any fun—how to enjoy a little risk?

Well, he'd show her.

He'd get her to smile no matter what.

He continued to rock the car, ignoring its squeak of protest.

But no matter how hard he shook—the smile never came.

His fingers slipped from the sides.

His car got away from him.

Swinging around, swinging upside down, until the rail came loose and dumped him right out.

The fall from one hundred feet went so much quicker than I ever would've imagined. And I watched as Satchel tumbled from his seat, arms flailing, legs kicking, head crashing and bumping its way from car to car until it finally smashed straight into the ground, where everything stopped.

Everything but the sound of Mary Angel's high-pitched scream.

A soundtrack that continued to play long after the

projector halted, the computer flipped off, and Satchel stood before me, head caved in on all sides, but worse at the top. His collarbone jutting right out of his skin, right through the big, gaping hole in his blood-soaked white shirt—his clothing battered, clotted with brain matter—just like they'd found him.

His one good eye burning into mine when he said, "So tell me, Riley, is that what you wanted to see?"

20

I had to say something.

He wanted me to say something.

I could tell by the way he'd removed the staples from my mouth and waited for me to speak.

Problem was, I wasn't sure where to start, so I went for the obvious. "Satchel, I'm really sorry about what happened to you, but you must know, it was an accident."

He rolled his one good eye, shook his battered head. A mouthful of cracked-up teeth spewing from his lips when he said, "Ya think?"

I pushed my bangs off my face and fought to stay calm, doing my best to get past his gruesome appearance, not to mention his uncalled-for sarcasm.

"What I meant was, it's unfortunate, yeah, but it's no excuse to do what you do. It's no excuse to terrorize people."

"What? Are you kidding? Did you miss something? I

mean, look at me, Riley! I ignored my parents' warnings, I lied, and look at the result!" He ran his mangled fingers up and down his body like a game show model displaying the prize.

The sight was miles past grisly, truly the stuff that nightmares are made of. But I couldn't afford to focus on that. I had to use whatever time I had left before he decided to dreamweave a whole new wave of terrors on my behalf. I had to find a way to get through to him.

Not wanting to waste another second, I yelled, "Stuff happens, Satchel! Really horrible, regrettable stuff. And while I'm sorry about what happened to you, and I really, truly am, I also have to be honest and tell you that I'm way more sorry about the way you lived your life before that. I'm sorry that you had no friends. I'm sorry that you didn't fit in. I'm sorry you never had a single moment of fun. But most of all, I'm sorry for the way your parents made you fear *every single thing*. I'm sorry they urged you to hide from the world. I'm sorry for all of that—far, far more than the sorry I feel for what happened to you at the fair."

My words silenced him. Caused him to stand before me, patting the caved-in mess where his hair used to be, oblivious to the small avalanche of flaky, dried blood that trickled down to his feet.

"I get that they loved you, I really, truly do. I get that you meant everything to them, and because of that, they were terrified of losing you. I get that they had your best interests at heart—only wanted to keep you out of danger. But by doing that, they made you a prisoner! Not being able to run, ride a bike, play sports with the other kids at school . . ." I shook my head, determined to not get too carried away. It was imperative to keep the message clean, clear, free of emotion—no matter how much his parents enraged me. "You had no friends, never experienced a single moment of real and true fun. And though it wasn't their intention, they turned you into a freak with no life. Heck, they wouldn't even let you have a pet—'animals are too dangerous,' they said—sheesh!" I paused, replaying my words and relating them to my own life.

Practically all I'd done since I'd died was complain about how short my life had been. Complained about what a bum deal I'd gotten when I found myself dead at twelve.

Until I met Satchel, it never even occurred to me to celebrate just how much living I'd done in such a short amount of time.

I'd had friends—lots and lots of friends.

I'd played sports—even though I wasn't very good.

I'd ridden my bike in the rain—laughing when the water splashed up from the back tire and drenched my sister, Ever.

I'd had a pet—in fact, I still do.

I'd had all the wonderful, normal life pleasures that Satchel has never once known. His parents had robbed him of them.

And I was suddenly so overcome with gratitude for all that I'd had—I could no longer mourn what I once thought I'd lost.

My life may have been ridiculously short—but the short time I'd lived had been pretty dang good.

"There are only two emotions," I said, returning to Satchel, unaware of what those two emotions might be until I actually stated them. "Love and fear. Love and fear is all there is—everything else is just an offshoot, motivated by those two."

I paused, wanting him to hear it, to get it, to completely understand what I was just beginning to understand for myself. Not really sure of where the knowledge was coming from and wondering if it might be the result of a thought-wave of some kind, but trusting it was true all the same.

"Only, in your family, love and fear got so confused they began to resemble each other. Fear got mixed up with love, until it began to *look* like love, to *seem* like love, to *feel* like love—when, the truth is, they couldn't be more opposite. I mean, think about it," I said, desperate for him to follow, to really listen. "Your whole, entire life, all thirteen years of it, the only time you truly felt alive was when you were riding that Ferris wheel, wasn't it? That's the only time you truly felt free—that's when you began to realize all of life's glorious possibilities. Though unfortunately, as we both know, you got a little carried away, and, as a result, things ended tragically. But I'm willing to bet that if you ever gazed down on the earth plane after you left, well, I bet you left one heck of a cautionary tale behind. I bet Jimmy Mac never shook a car on a Ferris wheel again. I bet he thought twice before he taunted someone he thought was beneath him. I bet Mary Angel never stopped feeling guilty about urging you to ride in the first place, which is pretty sad when you consider that the ultimate decision was yours, not hers—not to mention how she begged you to stop and you wouldn't listen. And I bet your parents really, really missed you. I bet they also held themselves responsible since you played right into their very worst fears. Do you ever check in on them? Do you ever . . ." I gulped at the thought but forced myself to continue, "Do you ever . . . make dreamweaves for them?"

He patted his head again, and I looked away. I really wished he'd stop doing that.

"Never! No! Sheesh!" he said.

I waited for a moment, hoping he'd say something more, but when he didn't, I took another leap, hoping it might work. "The thing is, Satchel, all of that happened a really long time ago, which means some of them are probably

Here now. Have you ever considered venturing out, out of this room, to see if they are?"

He looked at me, well, one eye did. The other was reduced to a black pit with long strings of cruddy bits streaming out.

"Are you kidding? I can't go out there looking like this!" His voice was tinged with hysteria, fear. "My parents will *kill* me! They must be furious with me for what I've done!"

I could hardly believe it. After all those years spent scaring an untold number of dreamers across the globe, after all those years of reigning supreme over their very worst nightmares, Satchel was still afraid of how his parents might punish him for his death.

"First of all," I said, trying to stick to the obvious, keep to the facts. "No one can *kill* you. In case you've forgotten, you're already dead. And second—don't you think it's time you guys had a talk? I mean, I could be wrong, but I'm pretty willing to bet they'll be overjoyed to see you again. And third—" My eyes fixed on his mangled hand that was in transit, just about to pat at the grotesque crevice in his head, turning in a way that made his jutting collarbone scrape a big chunk of skin right off his chin. The bloodied, battered bit hanging by a long string of *ick*, that swung up and down, back and forth, causing me to say, "You have *got* to *stop* doing that. Seriously, not only does the sight of it make me want to hurl, but there's really no need for you to look like this anymore. It's time for you to leave your past behind and head toward your future, don't you think?"

While I felt I'd made a pretty good case, he wasn't entirely convinced. He listened, considered, I could see it in his one, semi-good eye, but he was definitely teetering. He needed more proof.

Satchel had grown so used to his views, the fearful ideas his parents had drilled into him, that it was hard, if not impossible, for him to see another way. And there's no doubt that having felt so powerless in life, he'd come to enjoy the power he wielded over all those unsuspecting dreamers. As far as he was concerned, it was a lot to give up.

Dreamweaving was his life. *Er,* make that his *after*life. Without it, he had no idea what to do with himself.

Kind of like how I was with Soul Catching.

But if it was time for me to make a new start, then it was definitely time for him too.

We locked eyes, and I knew if I didn't say something quick, something positive, upbeat, and encouraging— something that would give him the final push that he needed—well then I'd lose him completely.

And while I had no idea what I might say, I decided to trust that the right words would find me—just like they often did when I was in the middle of a Soul Catch.

But this was no Soul Catch—or at least not officially anyway. Once again, I'd barged in where I didn't belong. I'd taken on a case without the Council's consent.

Which means the second I opened my mouth, the only sound that came out was a horrible croak.

A horrible croak that was soon followed by a high-pitched gasp when Balthazar stepped out of the shadows and made for the stage.

He strode toward me, dressed in the exact same uniform he'd worn earlier—the buttons on his shiny blue shirt still threatening to pop, his knee-high boots tapping hard against the floor, and I couldn't help but wonder just how long I'd been there. Had Dreamland officially opened for business again—or had Balthazar sensed some sort of trouble and come straight from his bed?

He looked at me, his gaze holding more warmth than I would've expected when he said, "The boy is not ready. These things cannot be forced."

That's what you think.

I turned toward Satchel, eager to prove Balthazar wrong, but all I found was an empty space where Satchel once stood. And no matter how long I stared, it only confirmed what I already knew—Satchel was gone.

I whirled on Balthazar, furious with him for interfering,

for butting in at the most crucial moment. I mean, seriously—if anyone should understand the concept of delicate timing it should be him. Hadn't he just spent an entire afternoon lecturing me about the importance of timing, of getting the landing just right? And yet, when it came to the scene *I* was directing, he just stormed right in without a thought.

"This is *your* fault!" I yelled, my voice containing a fury that surprised even me. "He was *this* close to changing!" I thrust my hand toward him, pinching my forefinger and thumb closely together. "I'd almost convinced him—and I would have too—I definitely would have—if *you* hadn't barreled right in and wrecked the whole thing!"

My cheeks grew hot and flushed, my throat grew all lumpy and hoarse, as my eyes stung from the threat of crystalline tears. Hardly able to believe just how close I'd come—only to lose it all in an instant.

But I didn't cry. Instead I turned to the side and blinked and blinked until I was ready to face him again.

"Don't you get it?" I said, my voice still shaky. "Satchel was my big chance! He was my big opportunity to advance myself straight into being thirteen! And I was so close—I was almost there—until you came along and wrecked everything." I shook my head, swiped a hand across my eyes. "You just had to butt in, and now . . . and now I'm right back where I started. Stuck as a scrawny, little twelve-year-old kid!" I stared at my feet, waving my hand before me as though erasing the words. There was no point in continuing, no point in anything. And as far as Balthazar was concerned, well I was really and truly over him. Everything bad could be traced back to him. If he'd just let me have my dream jump like I'd asked from the start, then the whole mess with Satchel never would've occurred.

I'd be back home, safe in my bed, dreaming sweet dreams after having gotten some good and solid advice from my sister.

But *nooooo!* Thanks to Mr. Skunk Hair, I was right back where I started, which was pretty much nowhere at all. Feeling so disgusted with myself and my stupid, level 1.5, barely there glow, I tugged hard on my sleeves, yanking them over my knuckles and down past my fingertips so I wouldn't be reminded of just how far I had to go.

Then I unstuck my bolted-down feet and made for the doorway.

Stopping just shy of it when Balthazar said, "You think I ignore Satchel? You think I did not try to speak with him, to reason with him? You think that you are the only one who has failed with the boy?"

I stood very still, thinking: *Um, yeah, that's pretty much exactly what I thought.* It never even occurred to me that there might be others who knew what Satchel was up to. But it's not like it made a difference. It was what it was.

"Dreamland is my creation, and at one time Satchel was my number-one apprentice," Balthazar said, an unmistakable hint of pride in his voice. "Nothing can happen here that I am not aware of."

"Then why haven't you stopped him?" I turned, but the second my eyes met his, I already knew. Free will, it ruled everything.

I shook my head and moved for the doorway. Removing the first slat and placing it on the floor when he said, "You know, Riley, you will never turn thirteen this way." I glanced over my shoulder just in time to catch the concerned look that he shot me.

"Oh, yeah?" I grumbled, grabbing the next slat and hurling it toward the ground. "Well, that's just *great*, Balthazar. Seriously. Thanks for sharing that. Thanks for the really useful, super-duper handy tip."

I frowned, blew my limp blond bangs out of my face, and removed the last remaining slat, eager to put some serious distance between us.

"This is not how you grow older. Winning is not all that you think it to be."

"Oh, yeah? So just exactly how is it done then?" I asked,

my voice thick with sarcasm, while the rest of me secretly hoped he might tell me.

"The way you grow older is . . . well, by growing older." He nodded as though he'd just made some huge revelation.

I groaned, rolled my eyes, thinking: *More useless words of wisdom from the great director himself!* Then I ducked down low and placed one foot solidly on the outside.

"You have so much potential, but no idea how to channel it," Balthazar said.

The next step came slower, I'm embarrassed to admit, but I was curious to see where he was headed with that.

"If you were not already apprenticing as a Soul Catcher, I would ask to train you as an assistant director. You are full of heart and fire. Every time you speak, I expect to see hot flames shooting out of your mouth."

Okay, I know I was supposed to be mad, but I couldn't help but smile at that. It wasn't entirely kind, but still, there was no denying it described me to a T.

"You also seem to have a fondness for ignoring the rules. Like the Dreamland closing time, for instance?"

My smile faded. And since I had no intention of sticking around for yet another lecture, I ducked and crouched 'til I was on the other side of the doorway. Already headed for the gate when Balthazar came after me, saying, "You have the soul of an artist. All great art is about bending rules—discovering a new way to blaze an old trail. You approach your afterlife with fierce determination and passion, and you love to win more than anything else. Qualities that must come in very handy in your job as a Soul Catcher, but, as you see, some souls will always choose to go their own way. It is just how it is. It bears no reflection on you."

I gulped. I couldn't help it. I guess I'd never thought of it that way. I figured the Council had made me a Soul Catcher because I could relate to the ghosts—because I knew firsthand what it's like to cling to the earth plane, the old way of life, refusing to move on to where I truly belonged. But maybe they saw something more in me too. Maybe my fire and heart and determination and passion and desire to win above all . . . well, maybe that had also played a small part in why I was chosen to do what I do.

My thoughts were interrupted by Balthazar saying, "And while these are very good qualities to have, one must learn to direct and channel them in order to achieve greatness. Without focus, they are just a pile of emotions left to run amok. It is the ability to channel one's emotions that is the mark of maturity, no?"

My jaw dropped, while the rest of me stood as frozen and solid as . . . well, as a snowman. Suddenly understanding it—or at least part of it—feeling as though I'd just been handed one more piece to the puzzle.

Balthazar tilted his head back, peering up at a sky that while still mostly dark, showed hints of silvery brightness beginning to creep in—the promise of daylight to come. Then he looked at me and said, "There's still some time before Dreamland officially opens for the day." His fingers worked the silk scarf at his neck. "What do you say we check in on that sister of yours?"

21

The scene was perfectly staged. My landing was spot-on. And yet, despite all of my preparation and training, it still took several tries to get it just right.

Ever kept running. Waking. Bailing on every happy scene I fought so hard to share with her. Forcing me to play out the same routine again and again—always starting with her laughing and smiling and pretending to go along—and ending with her running off the second I'd turn my back—scrambling for the surface—determined to wake herself up.

"What am I doing wrong?" I called, standing on the stage, voice full of despair, squinting at Balthazar, who was perched in his fancy red director's chair.

He shrugged, clearly not half as upset as me, saying, "You have done everything right. Just like I taught you. But also like I taught you, there are no guarantees. Sometimes a dream jump just does not work. And while usually it is the fault of the jumper, in this case, considering that you were personally trained by me, the blame clearly lies with your sister. For some reason, she prefers not to see you."

I stood there, stunned, speechless, knowing all the evidence seemed to support what he said, and yet, there's no way it could possibly be true. Ever loved me! She missed me! I knew it for a fact—despite how it may have looked.

Yet, I also knew that Balthazar was right, there was no doubt she was doing her best to avoid me.

"She is troubled. Feels very guilty about something. And your presence only seems to make it worse. She is convinced she is not deserving of the happiness that the sight of you brings."

Omigawd, that's it! Balthazar had just perfectly described my sister—the sole survivor of the accident that wiped out my family.

Still, I was determined to get through. I had no idea when the chance might come again. "One more time," I pleaded. "I mean, we still have time, right?"

Balthazar quirked his brow, stroked his goatee, and I took that to mean that the choice was entirely up to me. So the moment my sister fell back to sleep, I jumped. Only this time, instead of distracting her with laughter and fun, I let her lead the way.

She was troubled, immersed in a dark and lonely

landscape. And, if I didn't know better, I'd think for sure Satchel was behind it. But Satchel was nowhere to be found, which meant the scene we found ourselves in was, unfortunately, the wisps and remnants of my sister's guilt-ridden mind.

I went along for a while, but it didn't take long before I started to feel really sad about the way she was still punishing herself for events that were beyond her control—for making choices that may have proved tough at the moment but that, eventually, would surely work out.

And that's when I decided to send her a thoughtwave.

I had no idea if it was actually possible to send a thoughtwave during a dream jump, since Balthazar had made it sound like an either/or situation, but I figured it was worth a shot. So, I closed my eyes, concentrated on letting her know just how much I loved and admired her—how I'd spent an entire lifetime wanting to be just like her.

And then, the strangest thing happened, that dark, gloomy sky started to brighten, the crisp, cold air began to warm, as that depressingly bleak landscape transformed into a sparkling patch of grass—a small island refuge from all of her darkness.

"Don't fight it," I urged, smiling so brightly it made my cheeks ache. "Please, don't run—please just sit here with me and try to enjoy this moment for however long it lasts."

She knelt beside me on the grass, her blue eyes narrowed in question before pushing through the doubt and giving way to happiness. She reached toward me, smiling as she moved to tweak my nose in that way my dad always did, but then halfway there she stopped, reconsidered, and instead, used the tips of her fingers to softly brush my long and scraggly bangs off my face.

"You're growing up," she said, her voice as soft and wonderful as I remembered it.

Though the words were not at all true, causing me to shake my head, saying, "No, no, I'm not. I'm just exactly the same as you left me. But I want to grow up. I really, really do. And I was kind of hoping you could help."

She sat back on her heels, her long blond hair draped over her shoulders, hanging down to her waist. "Riley Bloom? Asking for help?" She tossed her head back and stole a few moments to laugh. "Are you sure you're my sister and not some crazy imposter?" She tapped lightly on my forehead, stared hard into each eye.

And though I laughed too, willingly going along with the joke, I have to admit her words kinda stung.

It was true that I never asked for help, and maybe that was also part of the problem. The Council had told me to consult with them, and once again, I'd totally ignored it, chosen to go my own way. But those days were over. I was ready, willing, and completely and totally desperate to soak up any words of wisdom my sister could give me.

"Ever, I was hoping . . ." I mashed my lips together, gazed all around, knowing I needed to hurry, that she could wake at any second and my chance would be blown. "Well, I was hoping you could tell me how to be thirteen."

She squinted, her face gone suddenly serious, her hand lightly clasping mine when she said, "Thirteen just happens, Riley. It's not something you can force."

Yes, I was becoming all too aware of that, Balthazar had said pretty much the exact same thing. But while I knew she couldn't help me *become* thirteen, I thought maybe she could at least help me to act it, which in turn might spur things along.

"Okay, well, here's the thing," I told her, my fingers grazing over the crystal horseshoe bracelet her boyfriend gave her, the one she always wore. "Turning thirteen isn't something that will just *happen* for me. I'm—" I started to say *I'm dead,* but not knowing if she was aware of that in her dream state, I didn't want to startle her and possibly risk waking her, so instead I just said, "It's . . . different for me. It's something I have to learn how to achieve."

She shook her head, made a face of impatience, eager for

me to understand. "But that's the thing, you *can't* force it. Nor can you achieve it. It'll come when you're ready and no sooner, I'm afraid."

To be honest, that only made me more frustrated. It was all the same stuff I'd already heard. I mean, so far all I'd manage to get out of Bodhi, Balthazar, and now her were the same, vague, mostly unhelpful statements.

You can't force it!

You can't achieve it!

It happens when it happens!

Bipiddy blah blah.

Channel your emotions was the only solid lead that I had, but it wasn't enough. I knew there was more.

"I know you're in a rush." She nodded intently. "And I know you probably won't see it this way, but really, you should consider yourself lucky. You'll turn thirteen when you're ready, no sooner. Can I tell you a secret?" She leaned toward me until our noses were just millimeters apart. "When my thirteenth birthday came, I didn't feel the least bit ready."

Wha?

I leaned back, stunned. Remembering her thirteenth birthday so clearly—the party our parents gave her, the mad crush of friends that filled up the entire den until they spilled out into the backyard. Remembering how surprised

I was to see how boys had made the guest list for the first time in a long time. But mostly I remembered how badly I wanted to be a part of it all. How I kept making excuses to join them, and how our parents kept urging me to leave her alone, to leave her and her friends to their teenaged fun. Assuring me that someday I'd get a thirteenth birthday party too, and then I'd understand . . .

I looked at my sister, convinced she'd only said that to make me feel better. I mean, seriously, she was pretty much the picture of the teen dream come true.

"It seemed like suddenly, practically overnight, all of my friends were obsessed with lip gloss and boys." She arched her brow, flashed a quick grin. "And I felt like in order to fit in, I had to pretend I was into that too. The first time I slow danced at the seventh grade mixer, my stomach was so twisted with nerves I thought I was going to hurl on that poor boy's shoulder." She laughed, flicked her fingers through her hair. "But honestly, none of it really felt right until around age fourteen. Maybe even fourteen and a half. I pretty much just faked it 'til then. But you're nothing like me, Riley. You don't have a single thing to worry about. You were sneaking my lip gloss from the moment I started wearing it." She laughed and chucked me under the chin. "You're ready, I can tell. There must be something else that's holding you back."

So, that's it, I thought. She really didn't know any better than I what that crucial thing might be. And while that was all fine and good, I wasn't ready to end it just yet. Though I could see the grass starting to shrink, to creep in on itself, as her attention started to fade.

"What about boys?" I blurted, determined to squeeze as much out of the moment as I could. "And making friends? How did you do that so easily? How did you get everyone to love and admire you? How did you become so popular?" I asked, my voice frantic, all too aware of time running out.

She was distracted, losing focus, and I was pretty sure that I'd lost her when she returned to me and said, "Boys?" She grinned. "My baby sister wants to know about boys!" She tossed her head back and laughed. And even though I cringed at the word "baby," I didn't let on. I was too busy urging her on. "Well, for starters, never forget that they're just as nervous as you are. Remember when I told you about that dance and how I thought I would hurl? Well, what I didn't tell you is that the boy's hands were so clammy and sweaty he left two permanent sweat stains on my blue satin top. He totally wrecked it and it was brand-new!" She rolled her eyes, tucked her hair behind her ear. "They're cute, no doubt, but sometimes they act like such dorks. It takes a while for them to figure it out. Believe me, I know, my boyfriend's six hundred years old!" She quirked her brow and shrugged. "Just be sensible, Riley—just be yourself. And never, ever, allow yourself to lose your head over any of them, okay? As for making friends?" She smiled, butted her knee against mine. "Easy-peasy—isn't that what you say? The key to making friends is to *be* a good friend." She paused, allowing her words to sink in, but I hoped she wouldn't pause too long, I could feel the dream starting to fade. "And what was your last question? About popularity and how to get people to love and admire you?" She squinted, took a moment to consider. "Well, the thing is—you don't. Or, maybe I should say that it's really not something you can strive for because you'll just come off as a big needy fake. Just be your adorable, sweet, and sunny self, and I have no doubt that everyone will . . ."

The grass was disappearing, and when Ever saw it, her eyes filled with panic and fear.

I tugged on her hand, desperate to bring her back to me. And, for a moment it worked, because she looked at me and said, "Don't worry, Riley—you're going to be fine. But now, I'm afraid something very strange is happening . . ."

The grass slipped out from under us and we found ourselves back on the stage, and I took it as a sign that my part was over. It had been her dream all along. I was just the jumper. It was time for me to find a way to help her.

The stage continued to transform, and that's when I saw

just how dark and troubled my sister's world had become. She was all over the place, frantic, panicked, unable to take it all in, so I did my best to make her focus on only the most important symbols, the things she absolutely shouldn't miss. And though Balthazar and Mort had both warned me that you can never be sure which part of a dream the dreamer will actually remember once they wake up—for some strange reason I found myself hoping she wouldn't remember the earlier part. I hoped she'd remember all the dark and weird symbols instead—that's where the real message lived. I may not have understood it, but I knew it was important. I knew she desperately needed to see it.

So when Balthazar shouted, "Cut! She's awake! That's a wrap!" well, despite all my failures in Dreamland—I couldn't help feeling as though it hadn't been a complete and total waste.

I'd spent time with my sister. And I'm pretty sure I was able to help her as much as she had helped me.

22

By the time I made my way out of that soundstage I was glowing.

Positively glowing.

Or at least that's how I felt on the inside.

I may have failed at nearly everything I set out to do—there may have been a renegade dreamweaver still on the loose—but I'd done all I could. Until the Council decided to assign him to me, Satchel wasn't my problem to solve.

So, that was me—brimming with newfound confidence—buzzing with the promise of all that I'd learned—when I ran smack into Buttercup and Bodhi standing on the other side of the door.

I dropped to my knees, hugging an overexcited Buttercup tightly to my chest. His thumping tail, and crazily licking tongue on my cheek, telling me he was very happy to see me.

And after a while, when I knew I couldn't delay any

longer, I met Bodhi's gaze. His face was guarded, conflicted, much harder to read than my dog's, though I was pretty sure they didn't share the same enthusiasm.

I was pretty sure Bodhi saved his cheek licking exclusively for Jasmine, even though the thought of that pretty much grossed me out.

And while I knew I should say something to explain myself, he was the first to speak when he said, "So, I hear you tried to work another Riley Bloom miracle back there." His voice containing an unmistakable—*something*—I couldn't tell what, as he jabbed his thumb back toward the old, broken-down soundstage.

I didn't respond. I just got to my feet and motioned for Buttercup to follow as I worked my way toward the gate. Remembering the last time Bodhi and I had seen each other—when he'd caught me watching while he read poetry to Jasmine—and feeling that same rush of horrified embarrassment all over again.

I'd been feeling pretty dang good until he came along, and I marveled at how quickly his mere presence made me feel just the opposite.

"You know, lots of people have tried to get Satchel to stop." Bodhi walked alongside me, refusing to honor the silence like I was trying to do. "His guide has tried many times—too many to count, really. And Balthazar has been making regular visits since the nightmares began. Trying to talk some sense into him, pleading with him to change his mind. But, in the end, Satchel always refuses to listen. You shouldn't blame yourself, Riley. Satchel's just not ready to move on."

"But he *was* ready," I mumbled, grinding my teeth tightly together, remembering just how close I'd come—only to have him run off at the very last second.

I mean, yeah, I'd moved past it. Was fully committed to letting it go and not replaying the moment again and again in my head. But that doesn't change the fact that I truly had been on the verge of breaking through to him. If Balthazar hadn't barged in, I could've, once again, been the one to succeed where all others had failed.

My eyes slewed toward Bodhi's, seeing the way he studied me, the way he thumped his chewed-up green straw softly against his stubble-lined chin.

"How'd you know to come here?" I asked, wondering if the Council might've alerted him—wondering just how much trouble I might be in. But it turns out it was nothing like that, Bodhi just shrugged and pointed at Buttercup, who gazed up at me, licked his chops, and twitched his pink nose.

"You know the Council will probably want to discuss this, right?" Bodhi said, and the way he spoke, I couldn't tell if it was a meeting he dreaded or anticipated.

I screwed my mouth to the side and crossed my arms over my chest, saying, "Well, I guess that's going to be pretty uncomfortable for you, then. So, my apologies in advance."

He quirked his brow, looked me up and down, and something about that got me so riled up it felt like my head might explode and blast right off my neck.

"And while we're on the subject of misdeeds," I said, staring him down with all that I had. "Let's not forget how you *lied* to me. You told me Dreamland was forbidden when it's *not*." I nodded vehemently, unable to remember if lying was one of the seven deadly sins, or just highly discouraged—but either way, I knew it was bad.

"I did what I had to," Bodhi said, his gaze about as guilt-free as it gets. "And sorry, Riley, but I won't apologize for that. You know, you're not the easiest person to deal with. I have no choice but to exaggerate just to get you to listen. But, as you can see, it still doesn't work. You do whatever the heck you want, regardless of what I tell you."

I stopped in my tracks, taking a moment to glare at him before I said, "Yeah, and because of that, there are a whole lot of ghosts out there who've crossed over!" I shot him a scathing look—the stink-eye at its very worst. "So, tell me, Bodhi, doesn't it bother you that *I'm* always the one who gets the souls to move on?"

I tapped my foot against the ground as his eyes narrowed even further, becoming two slashes of green.

"I mean, I hate to be the one to remind you, but let's not forget *I* was the one who got congratulated by Aurora, who we both know is pretty much the Council's president, or prom queen, or . . . whatever. Anyway, the point is, like it or not, I'm pretty much on my way to surpassing you. It's just a matter of time until you're stuck gnawing on your straw and squinting into my dust, wondering how you got left *so* far behind."

"Riley—" He lifted his hand in a lame attempt to stop me, but he should've known better. I'd only just begun.

"You think you're so *cool,* you think you're so . . ." My voice broke, but I forced myself to continue. "You think you've got *everything,* don't you? Just because you have a pretty girlfriend named *Jasmine*—just because you're fourteen—that doesn't make you better than me. Because you just wait, I'm about to turn thirteen any second now, I'm starting to figure it out, even though you've been refusing to tell me—even though you're determined to keep me stuck where I am. And then, once I am thirteen . . ."

He was no longer listening. Instead, he motioned toward something he wanted me to see, something that made his gaze grow so sad and regretful he was reluctant to look at me.

And when I swung my head in the direction he was pointing, I froze in my tracks.

My words stalled.

My eyes nearly popped from my head.

My mouth hung silent and long.

Dreamland was in full swing, open for business again, and some prop guys were moving a mirror to a soundstage that must've needed it for a dream jump. They paused right before me, stopping to chat with some other prop guys who were leading a group of camels, two zebras, and one elaborately painted elephant in the opposite direction.

The mirror shining so clean and bright—causing my reflection to glint in a way I couldn't deny.

I moved closer. Moved so close it fogged up in small patches when I blew on it. Tracing my fingers over my reflected contours, wondering just what exactly had gone so terribly wrong.

I'd survived a long night of terror, which had surely left its mark, but this had nothing to do with that.

It was my glow that left me speechless.

It wasn't shining brighter. In fact, it was barely shining at all.

It had dimmed.

Significantly dimmed.

While Bodhi stood beside me, glowing brighter than I'd ever seen him. His usual green nearly edged out by blue.

And that's when it hit me.

That's when I knew.

The stubble on his chin—the aqua glow that surrounded him—he'd bumped up, surpassed me.

He'd turned fifteen—while I was still twelve.

"It's not fair!" I cried, my face a raging mess of crystalline tears and red cheeks, the reflection vanishing the second the prop guys shot me a worried look and hurried away.

"*I'm* the one who does all the hard work! *I'm* the one who at least tried to convince Satchel to stop weaving nightmares! I put myself at great risk—while you—*you*—" I could barely stand to say it, but I made myself anyway. "While *you* lounged around in a garden, reading poetry to your *girlfriend!*" I shook my head, my throat so hot and tight I had to force the words to come. "So tell me, oh mighty guide of mine, tell me, *how is that fair?*"

Instead of answering, Bodhi stepped away. Taking Buttercup with him, trying to give me some space. Then, once I'd calmed down enough, he circled back and said, "The glow isn't solely determined by what you *do,* Riley." His gaze fixed on mine, and there wasn't a trace of triumph in it—at least I could be happy for that. "It's not about what you *accomplish*. It's never been about that—I thought you understood?"

"Then what is it about?" I said, my tone striving for venom, but landing on weak and pathetic.

"It's about what you *learn* while you're doing it. And, I hate to say it, but you've failed to learn one of the most important lessons of all."

I sank to my knees, hiding my face in Buttercup's neck. Overcome with embarrassment and shame, regretting my outburst in a very big way. It was the immature reaction of someone much closer to ten than the age I wanted to be— I'd done the opposite of what Balthazar had told me.

Instead of channeling my fire and passion and determination—I'd succumbed to them. I'd let my emotions control me. I guess understanding the concept and acting on the concept were two different things. Clearly I wasn't thirteen, because I was neither worthy nor ready.

"For someone who's so wrapped up in appearances, and don't even try to deny it, because you know you judge people by the way they look all the time—what is it you called me when we first met?" He looked at me, wanting me to say it, wanting me to engage in some way. Wanting me to admit that, yeah, I did, and sometimes still do, refer to him as dorky guy. But I refused. I didn't want to play. I wanted it to end. I wanted the whole humiliating talk to be over and done with so I could be on my way.

"Anyway, I think we both know what you called me, the point is—" He paused in a way that told me this next part was important, something he really wanted me to think about. "The thing that you really need to know is that *appearances are really just manifestations of how we see ourselves.*"

Huh?

I snuck a peek at him. He had my full attention.

"Thoughts create, right?" He waited for me to nod, to acknowledge him in some way, so I did. "And so, with that in mind, the way you see yourself, well, it has a direct effect on what you become, and how others see you."

I squinted, not entirely getting it.

"Take Aurora, for example. Aurora sees herself as not just a member of humanity—but as a *part* of all humanity. She sees absolutely no divide whatsoever, no boundary of any kind, between herself and everyone else. That's why you see the beauty of everything when you look at her. Her complexion is a mix of all the complexions, and her hair is the same, the way it transitions through the entire color spectrum and back again. But Riley, you're so stuck on being eternally twelve—as you choose to call it—you're so stuck in your anger, you're so determined to find a shortcut to get around it—that, in the end, you're just dooming yourself. By obsessing over it, you're keeping yourself stuck right where you are. The thing is, if you want to grow up, well, then you have to start *seeing* yourself as grown up. And, no offense, but you'll need to start acting like a grown-up too. Which means no more outbursts or tantrums. The bottom line is, if anyone's holding you back, Riley, it's *you*."

Ouch.

I'm not gonna lie, the words stung in a really big way. They also left me feeling really embarrassed, mortified, and ashamed—mostly because I could recognize the truth when it was jumping up and down and waving before me.

"You can't force it, Riley. You can't achieve it in the way you've been trying. In the Here & Now, there are no birthdays—you mature when you're ready."

I sighed. It's pretty much exactly what Ever said during the dream, still I looked at him and said, "But you once told me that if I keep up the good work, then I'll be able to transcend level one-point-five in no time! Was that another lie too?"

"No." He shook his head. "It wasn't a lie. That was and is one hundred percent true. But the thing is, you used to care about the souls you crossed over. You may have put yourself at risk, you may have gone off on your own despite my warning you not to, but the Council was willing to overlook all of that because it was clear that you truly cared about seeing those poor souls move on. And while I'm sure you eventually started to care about Satchel too, if for no other reason than his story is pretty dang sad, I think we both know you were mostly in it for what you thought it would get *you*. Your motivation was selfish, Riley, and I'm sorry, but there's no reward for that."

I stared at my feet, remembering just what had sparked the whole thing. Not having any friends, seeing him with Jasmine—it didn't seem selfish on the surface, but Bodhi was right. I'd only tried to help Satchel to benefit me.

"So that's why my glow dimmed?" I asked. I looked at him, my face clean and clear of all anger.

Bodhi dug his hands into his pockets, looking at me when he said, "It's the same as turning thirteen. It's not about achieving—it's about learning. You always see yourself as separate, like it's you versus everyone else, and everyone else better watch out because you have something to prove. But the thing is, we don't act alone Here, Riley. We work as a team—a community. A community you haven't even tried to be a part of because you're too busy looking for shortcuts and glory. And while your glow getting dimmer is not quite the punishment you see it as, mostly because there is no punishment Here, I'm sorry to say that, yes, your actions have caused your glow to regress. Though that's not to say that you can't get your glow on again."

My body went shaky, my eyes started to sting, but instead of crying like a big, fat baby, I gave Buttercup a good, tight squeeze and then I let him go free.

Making my way toward the gate once again, when Bodhi reached out to slow me. The feel of his fingers causing my whole body to tremble, making me feel all weird, like I had when I saw him with Jasmine.

"Riley—uh, I think there's more we need to discuss . . ."

I looked at him, saw that big, unbearable discussion sitting right there in his eyes, causing me to shake my head and wave it away.

No way, José.

No way would we talk about him and Jasmine and whatever they meant to each other.

It was stupid.

Dumb. Dumb. Dumb.

He'd just turned fifteen. I was still twelve.

There was absolutely nothing to talk about.

I picked up the pace, finding my way to the other side of the gate. Knowing it probably wasn't the most mature way to respond, but heck, it was better than a tantrum, and at least that was a start.

There was no doubt I still had a lot to learn. But there was also no doubt that I'd eventually get there. Sooner rather than later, that was for sure. I finally understood how it all worked.

Thanks to Balthazar, Ever, and Bodhi, the puzzle was complete—they had each donated a piece.

I had to channel my emotions—tend to the fire within so it wouldn't blaze out of control.

I had to ask for help when I needed it, tackle only the assignments that were given to me, and instead of focusing on how *I* would benefit from convincing the lost souls to cross over—I had to focus on how crossing them over would benefit *them*.

I had to quit focusing on being eternally stuck as a flat-chested, twelve-year-old kid—and instead see myself as the mature and confident teen I wanted to be.

I had to be patient, be a good friend—I had to be happy being me.

Arranging those items in a neat little list in my head, I couldn't help but smile at how good it felt to finally have a plan.

And even though I was still walking fast, there was no outrunning Bodhi when he was in one of his more determined moods.

He caught up to me, grasped my elbow again, and said, "Riley, listen, the other thing can wait, that's fine. Though I

.do need to know if we can leave now, or if there's anything you need to do first. Anyone you need to check in with, before we take off?"

I looked at him, staring into those deep green eyes. "What do you mean? Are we going somewhere?"

Seeing the way his face broke into a smile as he picked up a stick, tossed it high into the air, laughing as Buttercup leaped into the sky and flew after it.

Turning to me, a ghost of a smile still haunting his lips when he said, "I spoke with Aurora. The Council is sending us to Italy. Apparently there's a very stubborn ghost that's been haunting the Colosseum for several centuries. And since they know you've been itching for a challenge, they figured it was the perfect Soul Catch for you."

Coming in Winter 2012

Riley's adventures continue in
Whisper

The first thought that popped into my head when we entered the Roman city limits was: *Hunh?*

I squinted into the wind, droopy blond hair streaming behind me, feeling more than a little deflated as I soared over a landscape that was pretty much exactly the same as all the others before it.

My guide, Bodhi, my dog, Buttercup, and I had flown a great distance to get here, and even though flying was hands down our favorite way to travel, there was no denying how after a while, the scenery tended to get a bit dull—fading into a continuous blur of clouds, nature, and man-made things, all piled up in a row. And though I'd grown used to it, I guess I still hoped that Rome would be different, but from where we hovered, it all looked the same.

Bodhi looked at me, his green eyes taking note of my disappointed face, he shot me a quick grin and said, "Follow me."

He thrust his arms before him and somersaulted into a major free fall as Buttercup and I did the same. And the faster we spun toward the earth, the more the landscape below came to life—blooming with such vibrant color and detail, I couldn't help but squeal in delight.

Rome wasn't boring. It was more like the opposite—a city chockful of visual contradictions practically everywhere you looked. Consisting of a maze of crazily curving, traffic-choked streets that curled and swooped around newly renovated buildings and crumbling old ones—all of it looming over dusty old ruins dating back a handful of centuries—reminders of a long-ago history that refused to go quietly.

Bodhi slowed, his hair flopping into his face, when he nodded toward the ruin just below him as he said, "There it is. What do you think?"

Buttercup barked with excitement, wagging his tail in a way that made him spin sideways, as I gawked at the massive old amphitheater, marveling at its size and finding myself suddenly sideswiped by doubt.

I mean, yes, I'm the one who'd practically begged the

Council for a more-challenging Soul Catch—I wanted to glow brighter, and also turn thirteen more than anything else in the world, and I wrongly believed that excelling at my job was the one and only way to speed that along. But the longer I gazed upon that massive stone structure with its arches and columns and sturdy old walls—the more I took in its sheer size and scope—the more I thought about the activities it was known for: barbaric cruelty and slaughter, blood-soaked battles fought to the death—well, I couldn't help but wonder if I'd maybe been a little too ambitious, if I might've overreached.

Not wanting to let on to my sudden fit of cowardice, I gulped hard and said, "Wow, that's um . . . that's a whole lot bigger than I thought it would be."

Continuing to hover, my eagerness to land all but forgotten until Bodhi yanked hard on my sleeve and got us all moving again. But instead of leading us to the middle of the arena, he landed on the balcony of a very fancy restaurant, its all-white décor serving as the perfect backdrop to what may be one of the earth plane's most spectacular views.

He perched on the balcony's gray iron railing, gazing down at the landscape that loomed several stories below, while I sat alongside him, hoisting a not-so-cooperative Buttercup awkwardly onto my lap, his legs flopping over either side, as I said, "Do we have a dinner reservation I don't know about?" Knowing the joke was a dumb one, but I couldn't help it, nerves made me jokey.

Bodhi gave the place a once-over, taking in the spacious terrace filled with well-dressed diners enjoying elegant candlelit dinners and a sunset-drenched view that bathed the Colosseum in a glow of orange and pink—all of them blissfully unaware of the three ghosts sitting among them.

Then turning to me, he got down to business and said, "Okay, here's the deal, this ghost you're supposed to deal with—his name is Theocoles. No last name that I know of. And, please, do yourself a favor and call him by his *full* name. No shortcuts, no Theo, or T, or Big T, or—"

"I got it, Theocoles," I snapped, thinking it was certainly a mouthful, but it's not like it mattered, his name was pretty much the least of my concerns at that point. "What else?" I stared straight ahead, hoping to appear confident despite the way my fingers were twisting in Buttercup's pale yellow fur.

Bodhi squinted through his heavy fringe of thick lashes, his voice low and deep as he said, "According to the Council, he's been haunting the Colosseum for a very long time." I turned to Bodhi, arching my brow, in need of a little more detail, watching as he shrugged, then pulled a dented green straw from his pocket and shoved it in his mouth, where he proceeded to gnaw on it like a dog on a bone. "This guy is *intense,*" he continued. "He truly is a lost soul. He's so completely immersed in his world, he has no concept of anything outside of it, or just how many years have passed since his death, which, by the way, number into the thousands."

I nodded, giving Buttercup one last scratch on the head before allowing him to leap from my lap to the ground so he could go sniff all the diners and beg for table scraps—clueless to the fact that they couldn't even see him.

"Sounds like business as usual," I replied, with a little more bravado than I felt. While the Colosseum was certainly intimidating, nothing Bodhi had said sounded like all that big a deal. "Pretty much all the ghosts I've dealt with were intense," I continued. "And yet, I was still able to reach them, still able to convince them to cross the bridge and move on, so I'm pretty sure I can convince this Theocoles dude to cross over too. Easy-peasy." I nodded hard to confirm it, turning just in time to catch the wince in Bodhi's gaze.

"There's something more you need to know," he said, his voice quiet and low. "Theocoles was *the* champion gladiator back in his day. Feared by all—defeated by none."

"Did you say *gladiator*?" I gaped, thinking surely I'd misunderstood.

Bodhi nodded, quick to add, "They called him the Pillar of Doom."

I blinked, tried to keep from laughing, but it was no use. I knew the name was supposed to sound scary, but to me, it sounded like some silly cartoon.

My laughter faded the second Bodhi shot me a concerned look and said, "He was a *champion* gladiator. A real *primus palus,* that's what they called them, which, just so you know, translates to *top of the pole.* Widely considered to be the toughest, scariest, strongest, most fearless creature of the bunch. This is nothing to laugh about, Riley. I'm afraid you've got some serious work cut out for you. But then again, you did beg for a challenge."

My shoulders slumped and I buried my face in my hands, my short burst of confidence dying the moment the reality of my situation sank in.

I mean, seriously—a *gladiator*? That's the challenge the Council saw fit to assign me?

It had to be a trick, or maybe even a joke of some kind.

It had to be the Council's way of getting back at me for always ignoring their rules in favor of making my own.

How could I—a skinny, scrawny, semi-stubby-nosed, flat-chested, twelve-year-old girl—how could I possibly take on a big, strong, raging hulk of a guy who'd spent the better part of his life chopping his competition into small, bloody . bits?

Just because I was dead—just because he couldn't

technically harm me—didn't mean I wasn't quaking with fear. Because I was—I really, truly was. And I'm not afraid to admit it.

"I know it seems like a lot to ask of a fairly new Soul Catcher such as yourself," Bodhi said. "But not to worry, the Council only assigns what they know you can handle. The fact that you're here means they believe in you, so it's time you try to believe in you too. You have to at least try, Riley. What is it Mahatma Gandhi once said?" He looked at me, pausing as though he actually expected me to provide the answer, and when I didn't, he said, *"Full effort is full victory."* He paused again, allowing the words to sink in. "All you can do is give it your best shot. That's all anyone can ever ask of you."

I sighed and looked away. Believing in myself was not something I was used to struggling with—if anything, I bordered on dangerously overconfident. Then again, the situation I faced wasn't the least bit normal, or usual for that matter. And even though I knew I'd asked, if not begged for it, I still couldn't help but resent the Council just the tiniest bit for indulging me.

"And what about those other Soul Catchers?" I asked. "The ones who were sent before me and failed? I'm assuming the Council believed in them too, no?"

Bodhi chewed his straw, ran a nervous hand through

his hair, and said, "Turns out, it didn't end so well for them. . . ."

I squinted, waiting for more.

"They got lost. Sucked so deep into his world that they . . ." He paused, scratched his chin, and took his sweet time to clear his throat before he said, "Well, let's just say they never made it back."

I stared, my mouth hanging open, empty of words.

I was outmatched. There was no getting around it. But at least I wouldn't have to go it alone. At least I had Bodhi and Buttercup to serve as my backup.

"But please know that Buttercup and I will be right here if you need us. We're not leaving without you, I promise you that."

I looked at him, my eyes practically popped from their sockets, my voice betraying the full extent of my hysteria when I said, "You expect me to go in *alone*?" I shook my head, unable to believe how quickly things had gone from very, very bad to impossibly worse. "I thought that as my guide, it was your job, not to mention your duty, to *guide* me. And what about Buttercup? Are you seriously telling me that I can't even bring my own dog to protect me?"

I turned, my gaze sweeping the restaurant until I'd ze-roed in on my sweet yellow Lab all crouched under a table, chewing on a shiny gold stiletto a diner had slipped off her foot. Reminding myself that historically speaking, he'd never proved to be all that great of a backup. When push came to shove he was actually more scaredy-cat than menacing guard dog—but still, he was loving, and loyal (well, for the most part), and surely that was better than going alone.

Bodhi looked at me, his voice full of sympathy when he said, "Sorry, Riley, but the Council made it crystal clear that this was *your* Soul Catch. Yours, and yours alone. They asked me to stay out of it, to supervise only, and leave you to work it out on your own. But we'll try to throw you a lifeline if you need it—or should I say *soul line*? And while I thought about letting you bring Buttercup along, for the company if nothing else, the thing is, thousands of wild animals died in that arena, and some of them are still lurking in ghost form. Being chased by a lion or a bear could be pretty terrifying for him since he doesn't really get that he's dead."

I squinted into the dying light, gazing at the long, rectangular space filled with rows of narrow, crumbling, roofless structures that sat just below us—yet another ancient ruin. From what I'd seen, Rome had no shortage of them.

"It'll be dark soon," Bodhi said, his voice softly nudging. "The sooner you get started, the better—and you might want to start there." He gestured toward the ruin just below us. "It's the Ludus Magnus." He looked at me. "One of the biggest, most important gladiator schools in Rome's history. Could be a good place to begin, get your bearings, get a feel for the place . . . you know, before you hit the arena."

The arena.

I gulped, nodded, and tried not to think about my fellow Soul Catchers who never made it back. I mean, if the Council thinks I can handle it, well, who knows? Maybe I can. Maybe they knew something I didn't.

So I pushed my bangs from my face, took one last look at my dog still gnawing that shoe, then pushed off the ledge. Hoping more than anything that the Council was right, that I really was capable of more than I thought.

But already betting against it, as I made my way down.

acknowledgments

I'm incredibly grateful to work with such an amazing team of talented people who help bring the Riley Bloom series to life—including, but not limited to—Jean Feiwel, Rose Hilliard, Jennifer Doerr, Eileen Lawrence, Jessica Zimmerman, Elizabeth Fithian, Mariel Dawson, Samantha Beerman, Angela Goddard, Bill Contardi, and Marianne Merola.

Thank you to Sandy, for more reasons than I could possibly list.

But mostly, thanks to my readers, for allowing me to live this incredible dream!

Questions for the Author

In what ways are you similar (or different) to Riley Bloom?

Actually, Riley and I share a lot in common. I know what it's like to be the baby of the family, and though I hate to admit it, I've also been known to hog the microphone while playing Rock Band on the Wii!

How do you come up with your characters?

Honestly, I'm not really sure! The story idea usually comes first, and then as I'm busy working on all the ins and outs of the new world I'm creating, the cast just sort of appears.

What was your inspiration for the Here & Now, the magical realm where Riley lives?

Back when I first started working on the Immortals series, I did quite a bit of research on metaphysics, quantum physics, ghosts, spirits, and the afterlife, etc., all of which sort of fed into the concept of the Here & Now. I guess, in a way, it's how I hope the afterlife will be.

Do you believe in ghosts?

In a word—yes. I've definitely experienced enough unexplainable phenomena to ever rule it out.

Did you grow up with an older sister the way Riley did? How many brothers and sisters do you have?

I have two older sisters, both of whom I completely idolized. There's a bit of an age gap between us, one is ten years older, and the other five years older, and trust me when I say that I did my best to emulate them. I listened to their music, watched their TV shows, and read their books—all of which was way more appealing than my own, more age-appropriate stuff. And like Riley, I used to try on their clothes and makeup when they were out with their friends, though I suspect that revelation will come as no surprise to them!

Where do you write your books?

I have a home office where I put in very, very long hours seven days a week—but I have the best job in the world, so I'm not complaining!

Have you always wanted to be a writer?

Well, first, I wanted to be a mermaid, and then a princess, but ever since sixth grade when I finished reading my first Judy Blume book, *Are You There God? It's Me, Margaret,* I decided I'd rather write instead. I'd always been an avid reader, but Judy Blume's books were some of the first that I could directly relate to, and I knew then that someday I wanted to try to write like that too.

What would you do if you ever stopped writing?

Oh, I shudder to even think about it. I truly can't imagine a life without writing. Though I suppose I'd probably start traveling more. I've traveled a good bit already, both when I was working as a flight attendant and just on my own, but there are still so many places left to explore. Oh, and I'd probably enroll in some art classes too—painting, jewelry making, crafty stuff like that.

What would your readers be most surprised to learn about you?

Not long ago, every time I finished writing a book I would celebrate by cleaning my house, which, I have to say, was sorely in need of it by then. But recently, I've come to realize just how very sad and pathetic that is, so now I get a pedicure instead (and save the housecleaning for another day)!

ENTER AN ENCHANTING NEW WORLD WHERE TRUE LOVE NEVER DIES . . .

While Riley's learning how to make her way in the afterlife, her older sister Ever is learning what it's like to be immortal back on Earth.

ISBN: 978-0-312-53275-8
$9.95 US / $10.95 Can

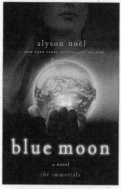

ISBN: 978-0-312-53276-5
$9.99 US / $10.99 Can

ISBN: 978-0-312-65005-6
$9.99 US / $10.99 Can

ISBN: 978-0-312-59097-0
$17.99 US / $19.99 Can

ISBN: 978-0-312-59098-7
$17.99 US / $19.99 Can

ISBN: 978-0-312-64207-5
$17.99 US / $19.99 Can

For free downloads, hidden surprises, and glimpses into the future visit
www.ImmortalsSeries.com

 St. Martin's Griffin